HUNTED AT WHITEFORD FARM

A Rolling Brook Novel

Blye Donovan

ISBN: 9798310450974
Imprint: Independently published
Cover Design by Central Covers.
Series Logo Design by K.B. Barrett Designs.

DEDICATION

To my husband, without you, this book never would have been written.

CONTENT WARNING

Contains profanity, mild violence, and mature sexual content. It also mentions the loss of a parent to cancer.

CHAPTER 1

Blair

The late afternoon sun warmed Blair's pale skin when she lifted her face to admire the clear blue sky. The call of a hawk drew her eye as it swooped overhead, searching for a midday snack. She smiled; the calm of nature soothed her, and all thoughts of the city—and a certain person in it—slipped away.

She'd pulled off the highway to explore this dirt road because it brought back memories of her childhood. As a girl, she'd spent summers on her grandmother's farm. She'd known they were getting close whenever her father had turned the car off the highway onto a dirt road. That farm had been a source of adventure and delight until the summer she turned seven.

Blair sighed; even the good memories brought in the bad. When she was seven, her parents divorced. Her mother took her to Chicago, and she hardly saw her father or her grandmother after that.

Kicking at a pebble, she wandered further down the dirt road. The sunlight glinted off the golden blonde waves of her hair. Tall pine trees lined each side, giving the road a secluded feel while spring flowers growing on the hillsides peeked through the leaves.

She longed to stop and smell them, but she settled for taking photos of them with her phone. There were brambles along the road, and she didn't have the right shoes on to venture into them. Memories flooded in as she snapped photo after photo.

She'd often picked wildflowers with her grandmother. The farmhouse had been surrounded by rolling hills covered in vibrant blooms, much like the ones she noticed rising beyond the trees on either side of the road.

Blair gazed at them, searching for the peace she'd felt only moments before. She needed this—a new beginning—and she was starting with fresh air.

Fresh air.

She smiled at the thought and inhaled deeply. The scents of pine and hay triggered more childhood memories of the time spent on her grandmother's farm. They made Chicago seem years instead of merely miles away.

Remembering the joy she'd felt running through corn fields and playing with baby goats helped overshadow the bitter fact of her current existence. Her whole life was in upheaval. She wasn't young anymore, and she'd wasted five years on a man who never had any intention of marrying her.

"Honk! Honk!" The sound of a car horn brought her

rudely back to the present.

She turned to find the honker bearing down on her much faster than the dusty 25-mile-per-hour sign warned.

Gripped with fear, Blair ordered her body to move, but her traitorous legs stayed unresponsive. She remained frozen to the spot in the middle of the tiny dirt road she'd wandered down, never thinking someone would actually still use it.

Even as she wondered about this, the car moved ever closer to her, not braking for her to get out of the way. Still stunned, she stared in horror as she faced her death.

This is how my life ends. Crushed by a silver Mercedes.

As she stared down the oncoming car, regret overtook her, and she found enough resolve to make her stiff legs move. Before she managed it, though, something slammed into her, knocking her to the ground.

Her breath whooshed out as rocks seemed to simultaneously stab her back and crush her front. The light dimmed, and the world shrank until, thankfully, she felt no pain.

"Dammit!"

The sound of a man cursing helped clear her tunnel vision. She realized the weight pressing the air from her lungs was actually a solid wall of muscle, not rock. Her panic subsided along with the faintness she'd felt.

His chest was firm, and even in her current state, the feel of him pressed full length against her was doing strange things to her body. Unfamiliar sensations bombarded her, attempting to break through the defenses she'd carefully constructed.

She kept her eyes closed as she fought this new experience from a complete stranger, no less. A tingle of fear danced down her spine. What would seeing the face that belonged to the body do to her?

Not ready to find out, she admonished the stranger without opening her eyes, "There's no reason to curse at me." Her air supply was running low. "By the way, do you think you could get off of me so I can breathe?" she huffed.

"Are you okay, miss?" the man inquired as he scrambled off of her. His voice became more insistent as she remained unresponsive. "Miss, can you hear me? Open your eyes if you're all right."

Blair braced herself, ready to meet the man who had saved her life now that he was no longer touching her and causing her body to react involuntarily.

"Hi," she answered while surveying the man crouched next to her.

He had dark hair worn a little long for her usual taste and the strangest shade of gray eyes she'd ever seen. His tanned skin was such a contrast to her pale complexion that she wondered at his ancestry. The rugged features of his face and the muscular set of his broad shoulders suggested a man who knew hard work—work performed in the burning sun, not in some cramped office with fluorescent lights.

He's the total opposite of Trevor.

Her expression soured as thoughts of her ex-boyfriend invaded.

"Are you hurt?" The stranger's question broke into her thoughts, and Blair was relieved that he'd stopped what was bound to be another mental tirade. She had some choice feelings regarding Trevor that she'd been trying to avoid thinking about.

At first, she wasn't sure if she *was* hurt. Pain had become familiar to her over the last few days, but she doubted this handsome stranger wanted to hear about her emotional pain.

"I'm not sure," she answered, frowning up at him.

"Can you move your limbs? Do they feel broken?" He bent down as though to examine her, and she fought not to smile at the panic that stole over his face when she continued to lie completely still.

Nothing was broken, but she felt the stinging of a scrape on her left arm. Her left elbow throbbed from its impact with the ground, and her leg on the same side would likely have bruises later.

Watching him struggle to think of how best to handle her with a broken limb, Blair relented.

She extended her hand as she pushed herself into a sitting position. "Blair O'Rourke. Thank you for saving my life."

"Jake Redland." He accepted her hand, though he dropped it hastily, making her frown.

The contrast between his rough palm and her smooth one intrigued her. When their hands had clasped, a tingling sensation had started to spread up her arm.

"Why were you standing in the path of an oncoming car, and why didn't you move?"

So much for hoping he'd accept my gratitude and be on his way.

Wondering how to answer him without seeming like a complete idiot, she cleared her throat to explain, "I thought the road was abandoned. The sight of the car took me by surprise. Plus, that car was going a lot faster than 25 miles per hour, or I would have had more time to react."

"Miss O'Rourke, you still haven't answered my question. What are you doing out here? This isn't exactly Chicago." Jake stared her down, and she was certain the man was used to people crumbling under the weight of that stare.

"Actually, I was out for a walk, more or less just wandering," she replied breezily, proud of herself for managing to speak calmly in the face of his obvious frustration.

"Why?"

"Do you think it would be possible to continue this conversation in, let's say, more comfortable surroundings?" she raised the question with a saccharine smile as she glanced nervously down the road in the direction the car had gone.

What if it came back?

"All right, I live close by. We can continue this *conversation* there." Jake's tone verged on hostile, and the thought of going anywhere with him made her uneasy. Thankfully, her reservations were clear on her face because he amended his demand. "Sorry, bad idea. How about I walk you to your car?"

Relieved, she blew out a breath and agreed, "Okay, but I'm not sure I know where it is."

Jake closed his eyes with an audible sigh. Then he opened them and stood in one fluid motion, offering her a hand up.

Wary of touching him again, she stared at his palm, afraid of experiencing that tingling sensation again. It would be rude not to accept, though, and honestly, she wasn't sure how steady her legs were.

Deciding she'd deal with the consequences later, she placed her hand in his, and he lifted her effortlessly to her feet. Standing next to him, she realized how tall he was. He had to have a foot on her five-foot, four-inch frame.

She began brushing the dust off her designer jeans and didn't notice Jake was already yards ahead of her. He'd started walking in the direction of Pine Tree Lane.

"Where are you going?" she shouted.

He turned around, his jaw clenched. "Look, lady." He seemed to catch himself and continued in a gentler tone. "Miss O'Rourke, I told you I'd walk you back to your car."

She propped her hands on her hips, her frustration getting the better of her. "Yes, I know that. What I'd like to know is why you're headed in the opposite direction than the one in which I arrived?"

"Because," he answered as if worried she wouldn't understand, "the way into this area by car is from Pine Tree Lane, the one I figure you followed to get here." A dark eyebrow lifted. "Am I wrong?"

She wanted to shout at him, "Yes!" but she reigned in

her temper. Once free, the results could be disastrous, and right now, she needed his help. "No, I do remember driving down Pine Tree Lane."

"Okay, then, if you come with me, I should be able to get you back to your car." When he turned around, she reluctantly followed, mumbling about patronizing men as she went.

* * * *

Jake

The Lexus drove away, and Jake cursed himself for not getting more information out of the woman. Maybe she *had* wandered from Pine Tree Lane since it was the only turn-off from the main highway, but he still didn't have a clear answer as to *why* she'd been on his land.

He assured himself that he wouldn't have been so accommodating if not for the hastily hidden vulnerability he'd seen flash in her eyes when she'd stared after the car that almost hit her.

Judging by her looks, he'd been sure he was going to be burdened by hysterics, but the woman had been cool and calm after nearly being mowed down by a silver Mercedes. That fact had sparked his frustration but also grudging admiration.

Why was the Mercedes on my property?

To anyone not familiar with the area, Pine Tree Lane seemed like the only entrance to Whiteford Farm from Route 30, but the fact that the car had come from the opposite direction was unsettling. He found it hard to believe the Mercedes was after the woman, but it hadn't seemed like merely an accident.

It was a good thing he'd been surveying the fences nearby. He shook his head, still confused as to why Blair hadn't moved out of the car's path.

At least he hadn't injured her when he'd had to knock her out of the way. She looked fragile with all those delicate features and her petite frame. Her eyes, though, had been anything but. They were a dark shade of green with little flecks of gold. He'd been attracted to the way they'd seemed to shift with each new emotion she'd let play across her face.

What am I doing, mooning over her eyes?

The last thing he needed right now was to get worked up over a woman. No matter how pretty she was. He had too much other stuff happening in his life, and, as far as saving some woman too simple to move out of the path of an oncoming car, well, he couldn't have just stood there waiting for her to get hit.

She was a curious thing, though. He scratched at his chin. She didn't seem the type to be out for an afternoon hike. Her clothes were casual but expensive and she had "city" written all over her. It was what made him so defensive. Well, that and her attitude. He'd asked her a simple question and she'd evaded the answer.

Privileged.

That's what she'd seemed, and Jake knew the type. In fact, he'd dated it—almost married it. Until she chose Chicago over him.

His thoughts turned bitter thinking of his ex. He'd met

Diana on a job when he was working as a carpenter in the city. She was an interior designer, and he'd found himself entranced by her take-charge attitude and her eye for beautiful craftsmanship. She'd commissioned him to build a dining room table for one of her clients, and they'd spent the next three years working and living together.

When it was time for him to come home to Rolling Brook and take over Whiteford, he'd thought Diana would be by his side. But she'd balked at the thought of living in the "sticks," as she'd put it.

Jake cursed himself. All he needed was to get wrapped up in another relationship like that. City women didn't know how to appreciate the farm, and he imagined Blair would be the same.

It had been over a year since Diana left. Now, he was 35 and single in a small town where the dating pool was sparse. Jake sighed, kicking at the clumps of dirt in the road with his work boots as he started back to the fence where he'd tied his horse.

He needed to focus on the farm, not a chance encounter with a blonde beauty from Chicago. Trying not to wonder if he'd ever see her again, Jake stopped walking.

What was that?

The sun glinted off of something shiny strewn amidst the dirt. Bending down, he picked up a phone. It had a sleek black case with gold striping. When he turned it over, a selfie of Blair came onto the screen.

He didn't know whether to be annoyed or pleased at

the prospect of seeing her again. Either way, he'd have to try and return it to her. He doubted she'd leave town without it.

CHAPTER 2

Blair

"Ugh, you've got to be kidding me!" Blair wailed, banging her hand on the steering wheel.

She'd reached for her phone and realized it was no longer in her back pocket. Which meant she must have lost it in the tussle with Jake.

Mr. Redland. She mentally scolded.

No need to get familiar with the man. She drummed her fingers on the steering wheel out of frustration.

She'd planned to leave him and this quaint little town behind, but not if she didn't have her phone. She groaned as she realized it was too late in the day to go back and look for it now.

The only solution was to find a place to stay the night and return to the spot in the morning, hopefully avoiding Mr. Tall, Dark, and Handsome altogether.

She fumed at the fact the cliché actually fit him. The man was determined to get under her skin. He'd helped her find her car with ease, which only made her angrier that she'd gotten herself turned around.

Thinking about it, she glared out the windshield at nothing. As a lawyer, she was used to working in a man's world, and coddling on any level did not sit well with her. After saying a stiff thank you, she'd gotten in her car and headed away from Jake's infuriatingly helpful yet ruggedly appealing face.

Too appealing.

She stopped her thoughts from straying in that direction. No matter what Jake Redland looked like, she had no desire to see him again.

Ignoring the little voice that called her a liar, she stopped the car when she saw a sign for a bed and breakfast. The establishment looked decent enough. It was an old two-story, brightly painted Victorian, which oddly fit in with the town of Rolling Brook. Various historic buildings lined the whole main street, several more of which looked to be from the same era.

She'd always loved old houses. Her formative years visiting her grandmother's weathered farmhouse had never failed to spark her young imagination. History lived in the bones of old buildings. You never knew what you'd find hidden in a closet or tucked under a floorboard.

She grabbed her suitcase and carried it up the wooden steps, admiring the turned balustrade as she went.

The foyer had been turned into reception, though no one stood behind the delicately carved mahogany stand to greet her when she entered. She glanced around and admired the colored wallpaper, faux marble baseboards, and glistening hardwood floors.

Someone had gone to a lot of trouble to restore this place. The restoration was both welcoming and disconcerting. It felt as though she'd stepped into a museum. Fresh flowers perfumed the air from a pot by the door, and another set of stems graced a vase on the reception stand. They gave the house a pleasant scent of spring.

Distracted, taking in her surroundings, Blair jumped when the receptionist finally appeared.

"Why, hello! I hope you haven't been waiting long. Sorry if I spooked you," a short, plump woman in her fifties—Blair guessed—greeted her. "I thought I heard the door, but I wasn't expecting another guest tonight."

"I'm sorry, I don't have a reservation. Do you have any rooms available?" She nervously twisted her purse strap and hoped she wouldn't have to find somewhere else to stay.

"I do, yes. And how long will you be staying?"

Blair breathed a sigh of relief as the woman pulled a ledger from a shelf behind the stand.

"Just tonight," she hurriedly replied.

The woman smiled at her from underneath her reading glasses while writing Blair's information in the ledger. "Well, now, that's fine. Rolling Brook is such a great town. I do hope you get to see some of it before you move on."

She smiled politely in response. "Yes, me too."

When the receptionist asked for payment, she handed over her credit card and was mildly relieved to see a credit card terminal to complete her reservation. With the lack of a computer at reception, she'd begun to suspect that the B&B was handling transactions in keeping with its Victorian-period decor.

"Can you recommend a place for dinner?" Blair hadn't eaten since breakfast.

"Oh, sure! Right down at the corner is Shug's Diner. You can't go wrong there."

"Thanks." When the machine beeped at her, Blair retrieved her credit card.

"Here now, let me help you with your bag. You'll be in suite three. It's right at the top of the stairs." The woman grabbed Blair's luggage before she had a chance to object and started for the steps.

"Thank you, really, but I can carry that."

"Oh, it's no trouble. I've got it." She set Blair's bag in front of her room. "Here's your key. My name's Janet, and you let me know if you need anything. There's a bell at reception if I'm not around."

"Okay, thank you again," she said, taking the large brass key from the woman.

The room was as beautifully restored as the rest of the house. A large four-poster bed with a canopy occupied the bulk of the space. She imagined the curtains that once must have hung around it with a smile.

A faded peach area rug complimented the gold-threaded wallpaper and mahogany night tables. Though old, it felt luxurious. Blair couldn't help it; she flung herself on the bed.

It was softer than she'd thought it would be. The

mattress had to be a pillow top. She sighed in contentment, but her stomach growled, reminding her she needed to eat.

After a quick stop in the adjoining bathroom, where she let out a squeal of delight at the sight of a claw-foot tub, she made plans to try it out later. It had to help with the aches she was starting to feel from her near brush with the car.

First, though, she needed to check out Shug's and give her stomach the sustenance it demanded.

*** * * ***

Blair

The diner sat right at the corner, as Janet had said it would be. The building was small and surprisingly full. Blair had to squeeze through patrons to find a seat at the counter. The smells wafting from the kitchen were enticing, and she hoped the food would be good. After she sat, she skimmed the menu and settled on the Reuben sandwich.

"Hi, what can I get you?" asked a perky young woman with bright blue eyes. Her name tag read 'Daisy'; Blair thought it fit her.

"The Reuben, please, and a glass of water with lemon."

"You want fries with that?"

"Yes." Blair beamed. No need to skimp when she'd only had a yogurt today.

"'K. Be just a few minutes."

"Thanks." She scanned the diner while she waited and

noticed several curious glances in her direction. She supposed in a small town like this, everyone knew each other. Her grandmother would have said she stood out like a sore thumb.

Blair had never really understood that expression. Were people examining each other's thumbs for something once upon a time?

She let it go, surprised she kept thinking of her grandmother. This town really brought back memories. At least those were good ones. She hadn't seen her grandmother in twenty years, though, and she'd passed away more than ten years ago.

"Here you go." Daisy pulled Blair back to the present. The scent wafting from her plate nearly made her moan.

"Best Reuben in town," the older gentleman sitting next to her commented before she could take a bite.

She smiled politely but wasn't thrilled about the man delaying her meal. Not when she was ravenous. It'd be hard not to devour the sandwich like a starving dog.

Daisy laughed. "It's the only Reuben in town, Mr. Delacourt."

Blair kept her smile in place, but the desperation must have shown in her eyes because Daisy rescued her. "Now, you leave the woman be and let her enjoy her meal."

She nodded a thank you before tucking in.

Wow. It really was the best Reuben she'd ever tasted.

Halfway through, she started to slow down enough to feel chagrin for ignoring the elderly man earlier.

She turned to him with a smile. "You're right. Best Reuben I've ever had."

"Hank." He stuck out his hand.

She wiped hers quickly on the paper napkins, aware the dressing from the sandwich had dripped between her fingers. "Blair," she replied as she shook his hand.

"Well, it's nice to meet you, Blair. What brings you to our little corner of the world?"

"Oh, I'm just passing through. Or I will be once I retrieve my phone. I lost it earlier," she explained.

"It's a funny thing." Hank scratched at his forehead and knocked the cap on his head askew. "You never used to lose phones in my day. They were attached to the wall."

He said this with such consternation that she had to laugh. "No, I suppose you didn't have that problem before cell phones."

"Where'd you lose it?"

"Oh, well, it's, um, I think it's somewhere off Pine Tree Lane. I was walking through there, and it must've fallen out of my pocket." She tried not to mention the near miss with the car. She did *not* want to rehash that.

"Hmm, I see. Daisy here could probably help you with that."

Blair tried to stop him as Hank called the server over. She didn't need more people in her business, but it was too late. Daisy was already heading their way.

"Daisy, Blair here, says she lost her cell phone off Pine Tree Lane earlier. You think you can get that brother of yours to help her find it?"

Brother? Does he mean Jake? Is Jake Daisy's brother?

Blair's anxiety rose. Now that she really looked at the woman, she did see a resemblance. The same deeply tanned skin and dark hair. Though Daisy's eyes were several shades darker than her brother's, they were the same almond shape.

"Is your brother Jake Redland?"

Daisy's smile grew. "Yes, have you met him?"

"I have."

As Daisy stared expectantly at her, Blair felt the heat rising to her cheeks. She averted her eyes and hoped the woman wouldn't comment on the blush that colored her face.

"Well," Daisy offered when she didn't continue. "I'm sure he would go back out with you tomorrow and help you look for it. Here, I'll give you his number, and you can ring him. That is if you have access to a landline?"

"Oh, yes, I do, thanks." She waited while Daisy scrawled the number on a napkin. "I can call him from the bed and breakfast."

"Great. Here it is. Did you want anything else or to look at the dessert menu?"

"Thank you, no. Just the check is fine." Daisy set it in front of her, and Blair smiled politely, hoping that the awkwardness she felt about getting Jake's number didn't show on her face.

When Daisy walked away, Hank said, "Well, now see how that worked out. You gotta love a small town, Miss Blair."

"I guess you do, Hank. Thank you for your help." She left cash on the counter to cover her meal with a generous tip for Daisy.

The girl was sweet and open, whereas her brother

seemed reserved. Growing up an only child, Blair was hardly an expert on sibling dynamics, but it surprised her to see how very different they could be.

On her way out the door, she noticed the man in the corner booth openly staring at her. He was average-looking with brown hair and eyes. He seemed vaguely familiar, but she brushed it off, thinking no one she knew would be visiting Rolling Brook. A little unnerved by the exchange, she hurried out of the diner.

In the parking lot, she spotted a silver Mercedes and froze.

After several seconds, Blair shook herself. It was absurd to think it was the one that tried to hit her.

A lot of people drive the same car.

She started her trek back to the bed and breakfast, looking forward to soaking her battered body in a hot bath. Halfway there, her scalp prickled with the sensation of being watched.

She spun around quickly, but no one was visible. Spooked now, she picked up her pace, nearly running by the time she reached the corner where the bed and breakfast stood. The old Victorian loomed above her with its ornate woodwork and decorative trim catching the lamplight and casting misshapen shadows.

Scrambling quickly up the stairs to the wraparound porch, she placed her hand on the doorknob as a man stepped out of the shadows.

She jumped, barely managing to muffle a scream.

"I'm sorry." Jake raised both hands in apology. "I didn't mean to scare you."

Her breathing was labored, and she worked hard to steady it. "Where did you come from?" she demanded when she'd caught her breath. "Were you following me?"

"What? No. I've only been here a few minutes," he explained, irritation clear in his voice. "Janet told me you went out for dinner, and I was about to head over to Shug's."

"Oh." Blair wasn't as relieved by that as she thought she'd be.

Who was following me then?

"Wait, how did you know I was at the B&B?"

"This is a small town. It's the only place to stay apart from the Motel 6 out on the highway, and you didn't strike me as a motel kind of woman." Jake had the nerve to smirk at her.

Blair hummed noncommittally, not wanting to give him a chance to gloat at being right. "Why were you looking for me?"

"Because I found this. I figured you'd want it back." He pulled her phone out of his pocket, and she nearly wept with joy. In truth, she'd been worried about the odds of finding it.

"Thank you," she said, her voice heavy with feeling as she reached for her phone. Their hands brushed in the exchange, and the tingling sensation started again.

She looked Jake in the eye, curious if he felt it too. What she saw in his gaze made her breath catch, but the spark of desire she'd seen vanished as quickly as it had appeared.

He stepped back from her, the distance making her

shiver.

Of course, he noticed. "Are you all right?"

She wasn't about to admit the effect he had on her. Instead, she told him, "Yes, I think so. It's just . . . I thought I saw the same car that almost hit me parked at the diner. Then, on my way back here, it felt like someone was following me." She glanced over her shoulder again, still unnerved.

She figured Jake would think she was overreacting, so she was surprised when he said, "I didn't recognize the Mercedes on my land earlier. I don't think it belongs to anyone around here."

"Your land?" The words were out before she had a chance to think about them. She glanced away with a mumble, "I didn't realize."

"The road you were on is part of Whiteford Farm. It's been in my family for generations. One of my ancestors bought it after marrying a woman from the Cahokia tribe. We don't usually get visitors on that road, but now I had two in one day."

"Hmm," Blair murmured. So, he had Native American ancestry. She could see it in the tone of his skin and the shape of his eyes. When she realized she was staring, she shook herself. That's not what she needed to focus on right now.

What had he said?

If visitors weren't usually on that road, she was even more worried that the Mercedes had been following her. That meant she was likely right about someone following her tonight, also.

"I can ask Daisy about any other visitors at the diner. She'd know if they weren't local, possibly help identify 'em," Jake offered.

"All right," she grudgingly agreed. Accepting his help wasn't her strong suit.

"Okay, I'll tell you what I find out in the morning. That's, if you'll still be here?"

Blair didn't want to be, but she also wanted to know what was going on. It wasn't like she had anywhere pressing to be, so she decided to delay leaving, at least until the afternoon.

She was on a self-imposed holiday with no destination or return date planned. Eventually, she'd have to go back to Chicago, but for now, she needed time away.

"Yes, I'll be here. Thank you for looking into this for me."

"No problem."

"Goodnight." She was ready for that hot bath, and a glass of wine to calm the nerves this evening had sent buzzing.

"See you in the mornin'." Jake waved, and she couldn't help but admire how broad his shoulders were as he walked away.

Exasperated with herself, she sighed. Now was not the time to let herself be taken in by another man.

CHAPTER 3

Jake

As Jake walked to Shug's, thoughts of Blair filled his head. He understood why she acted so jumpy when he'd stepped into the light on the porch. If someone had followed her back to the bed and breakfast, they blended in with the shadows. He certainly hadn't seen anyone.

The Mercedes, having been at the diner, was curious, though. This was a small town, after all, and the locals didn't lean toward the shinier vehicles. Maybe it was another visitor, or maybe it really was the same car from earlier.

He hoped the vehicle would still be parked at Shug's when he got there. If not, he'd at least ask Daisy about any unfamiliar customers.

He told himself that finding out what the car was doing on his land was paramount. It had nothing to do with helping the polished blonde with the delicate skin and wounded eyes. He just wasn't sure he believed himself.

When he reached Shug's parking lot, the Mercedes was gone. He'd suspected it would be, but he also knew there was a camera on the corner of the diner pointed at the lot. Shug had installed it last year when young Jesse Laudabaker thought it was a good idea to steal the sound systems out of customers' cars while they ate their meals.

Dillon had a field day with that one. Jake supposed it was good to have a brother on the police force now and again. He was planning to leverage that familial connection to get a look at the camera footage and hopefully an I.D. off the Mercedes' plates.

Smiling at the idea, Jake stepped inside the diner. It was starting to clear out after the dinner crowd. He noticed Mr. Delacourt at the counter. Jake would swear the old man was always there. Every time he came in, Mr. D. sat on the same stool, ballcap slightly askew, hunched over the day's paper, even though he must have read it through by now.

With a wave to Daisy, Jake sat down beside Mr. Delacourt. "How are you, Mr. D.?"

"Hey, now, Jake. We were just talking 'bout you. Must've had your ears burnin'."

"Is that so?" Jake smiled and played along.

"Seems there's a visitor in town who could use your help. Pretty little thing. Blair was her name. Said she lost her phone."

"Yeah, thanks. I just gave it back to her." Jake scratched at his neck. "But she was kind of spooked when I saw her. She thought someone followed her back to Janet's. Did you see anyone in here that wasn't from town?"

"Hmm." The old man rubbed at his forehead. "Well, there was a fellow sittin' in the corner booth there," he said, pointing. "Come to think of it, he left right after Blair."

Troubled by this, Jake called to his sister.

"Hey, big brother. You want something to eat? Or perhaps some dessert to share with your new friend?" Daisy asked him ever so sweetly.

"Hah, no," Jake answered, used to her teasing. "But, Daisy, she thinks someone followed her back to the B&B. Mr. D. said there was a man in the corner booth, not from here. Do you remember him?"

Daisy scowled. "Yes, he was very quiet. Didn't say more than five words to me and left a horrible tip."

"What'd he look like?" Jake prodded her.

"Um, kinda average, I guess. Brown hair, brown eyes. He wore a suit, not a sharp one like the guys in *Ballers*. More like early *Law & Order*."

Jake resisted the urge to roll his eyes at his younger sister. Daisy loved television shows. Thankfully, he understood what she meant.

At least he had an idea of what the guy would look like if he happened to show up on the security camera footage.

Jake glanced at his watch. Dillon was off duty by now and not going to be thrilled with his need for a favor, but he had to ask. He wasn't sure why, but the woman had already captured his interest.

She was a mystery, and they didn't get many of those

in Rolling Brook.

Well, desire had something to do with it, too. When their hands had touched, he'd admired how soft and smooth her skin was, and he'd wondered at the feel of the rest of her. Though he hardly knew her, some primal part of him wanted to help her, claim her even.

She didn't seem the type to like that idea, which oddly made her more attractive. He told himself her reticence was a good thing. He was facing a potential court battle against the developer who refused to take no for an answer, and all his focus needed to be on the farm, no matter how much Blair stirred his blood.

Frowning now, Jake thanked Mr. D. and his sister and left the diner to track down his brother.

* * * *

Blair

Blair was nearly asleep in the deep claw-foot tub when her phone beeping roused her. She'd been so focused on the idea of a bath to soak her aching body that she hadn't even checked her messages.

Glancing at her screen, she saw the beeping was a voicemail from her ex-boyfriend. She debated whether to listen to the message or not. Her pride warred with her curiosity, but curiosity won.

"Blair, it's Trevor. Look, babe, I think you're in trouble. Men came to see me about some missing money. I know you never believed the rumors about him, but I think Marco Soldano sent them. I told them I didn't know anything about the money, but the fact you took off at the same time it came up missing . . . doesn't look good. Might want to watch your back."

The gall of the man! She seethed as all the calm she'd gained from her bath slipped away.

It irked her that it took her so long to realize Trevor was such a prick. But this? To accuse her of stealing money and from a purported crime boss, no less!

Agh! She wanted to hit him. No, better than that, she wanted to humiliate him the way he humiliated her.

They'd been together since law school, and she'd thought they would eventually get married. Trevor had been her first and only. He'd won her over with his persistence, and she'd fallen hard for his boyish charm and suave good looks at the ripe age of 24.

She'd thought they had the same plan. They'd graduated together, joined the same firm, and, five years later, were right on track for that all-important question until he proceeded to tell her it was over.

What a fiasco that had been.

Dinner at Chez Charles was her favorite, and she'd been sure Trevor picked the restaurant to propose, which is why she was certain she'd misheard him when the words that came out were not "Will you marry me?" but rather "I think this has run its course."

The nerve of that jerk!

She'd been so angry she'd thrown her half-eaten chocolate mousse right at his face. Her anger cooled, and a delighted grin spread across her lips as she remembered how he'd sputtered at that. She was definitely better off without him.

After that disastrous dinner, she returned to their apartment, packed quickly, and drove out of the city.

Now, mere days later, Trevor was telling her that her leaving like that had roused suspicion.

But why?

Blair struggled to comprehend what could have caused Marco to think she had anything to do with his missing money.

Oh no.

Her stomach sank. Anger was quickly being overcome by fear. What if Marco was already after her? It could explain the Mercedes.

Another worry tripped her pulse. Did he follow her back to the bed and breakfast?

She jumped out of the tub, sloshing water as she went. All thought of relaxation had fled. She wondered if she should leave, but she worried Marco might be out there right now, waiting for her.

On the verge of hyperventilating, she raced around the room, attempting to get dressed and pack her bag at the same time.

Looking down at the disarray her belongings had become, she made herself take a calming breath. After letting it out, she shut off the panic and focused her analytical brain on the problem at hand. Her ability to evaluate objectively in this manner led to her success as a lawyer.

But perhaps she'd been too successful, Blair thought now.

She was the one who'd defended Marco Soldano in an extortion case a year ago. Despite suspecting his guilt, the evidence against him hadn't held up. It had been an easy win getting the case dismissed. Soldano was a high-profile client of the firm she worked for, and she'd received ample praise for her efforts in the case. The partners wouldn't have asked her to represent him if he was an actual crime boss.

Would they?

She packed her toiletries and wondered if she should contact Marco because it was absurd for him to think she'd ever steal from him. Unless. . . unless Trevor made it seem that way.

Would he stoop so low?

A month ago, she never would have entertained the idea. Now, she wasn't so sure. But she wondered why her ex would have called to warn her if he'd set her up.

Oh, God! Suddenly, Blair understood why.

The phone.

It was issued by the firm, and all of them were tracked internally by their IT division in case of theft. She shut it off and dropped it in the tub of water.

Anxiety wanted to creep in as she heard the splash and watched it sink to the bottom. No way was she staying at the bed and breakfast now. But she only knew one other person in town.

Can I trust Jake Redland enough to stay with him? She cringed, not enjoying that option.

The smartest thing to do would be to flee, but if Marco's men were already here, already watching her, they'd follow her if she did.

What she needed was to find out if that Mercedes belonged to Marco.

She glanced at the phone in the tub again and realized she'd have to ask Janet for a landline.

CHAPTER 4

Jake

"Hello, Janet. Seems a little late for you. Is everything all right?" Jake asked into the phone, unsettled that the cheerful bed and breakfast owner was calling him at close to midnight. He tried not to yawn. After getting ahold of Dillon, it had been a long night for him, too.

"It's not Janet," the voice on the other line said. "Look, I need your help. How soon can you meet me at the bed and breakfast?"

Jake jerked upright in his chair, surprised to hear Blair's voice asking for help. "Five minutes." He didn't hesitate on the response. It would take even less than that at this hour to drive the short distance from the police station.

"Thank you. See you then." The line went dead.

He hung up the phone and looked into his brother's inquisitive face. The resemblance was obvious in the dark hair, the burnished skin tone, and the shape of his eyes.

But like his twin sister Daisy's, Dillon's pupils were bright blue and sharp as they scanned Jake's face.

"What was that about?" his brother asked.

"I have to go. That was Blair. She wants me to meet her at the B&B." Jake rose as he answered and headed for the door.

His legs were happy to stand again. He'd been sitting in that chair, staring at a computer screen with Dillon for the past couple of hours. They'd been reviewing the footage from the diner parking lot.

"Wait, do you want me to come with you?"

He knew why Dillon was asking. The footage had given them a clear shot of the unfamiliar suit leaving the diner right after Blair. The man had gone on foot, but less than half an hour later, he returned and drove away in the silver Mercedes.

It was suspicious but hardly damning evidence.

They hadn't been able to pull a plate number either. The footage was too hazy, which meant he still didn't know who was after Blair, but it did seem like someone was watching her.

"No, but keep your phone close," Jake told him. He didn't know what happened to make Blair call him, but he wanted to find out before he brought in the police and chanced spooking her off.

* * * *

Jake

"In here," Blair called from the front parlor as Jake

stepped into the bed and breakfast.

The hardwood floor creaked underfoot as he made his way toward her voice. "Why are you sitting in the dark?"

"Shh, not now," she pleaded. "Can you take me to your place? I can't stay here."

The desperation in her voice made him quick to reply, "Of course."

"Thank you. Let's go." She grabbed her bag and started walking toward the door.

"Wait. Why can't you stay here?" He tried to understand why this woman would want to suddenly go home with him when she seemed panicked at the idea only hours earlier.

"I'll tell you, but I need to get out of here first."

In the faint light coming in from the porch, he could see the fear shining in her eyes. Something had her severely spooked. She'd tucked her long hair into her jacket and covered the rest with a scarf.

He cleared his throat. Laughing was the wrong thing to do in this situation, but her look was comical. It screamed, 'I'm trying not to be seen,' and was straight out of an old Hollywood movie. All she needed was the oversized sunglasses.

"Um, maybe put this on." He offered her his ball cap.

"What? Why?" she asked, clearly not understanding how out of place she looked.

"I'm guessing you're trying to disguise yourself by the way you covered your hair?" When she nodded, he added, "Well, the look you've got going makes you all the more noticeable. You're trying too hard."

While she glared at him, he watched the flames of her temper ignite, reflecting in her unusual eyes. Before she burned him with it, though, he took the scarf off her head and replaced it with his cap. It was better but still not much of a disguise.

"Ready?" He reached for her luggage.

With a scowl, she waved for him to go ahead.

Once outside, he hefted her Louis Vuitton suitcase into the bed of his pickup. He didn't notice her wince at the amount of dirt it contained.

When she moved to climb into the cab, he held the door open for her. He saw she wanted to argue about the gesture, but she restrained herself.

Before he could offer to help her into the cab, she used the grab handle to boost herself in.

He smiled at her, aware of the game they were playing.

She sure is reticent about accepting my help.

As he walked around the hood of the truck, he chuckled at the irony of it, considering she'd called him for that exact reason.

When he'd climbed into the driver's seat, he started the engine and asked, "So, you want to tell me what's goin' on?"

Blair grumbled, "Drive."

Something in her voice kept him from poking at her. Instead, he did as she asked.

After they made it to the highway, she continued, "It's possible that Mercedes followed me here and that someone is watching me. Though I'm not sure how closely. Hopefully, they'll see my rental car at the bed and breakfast and think I'm still there."

"How do you know? What happened after I left?" Jake probed for more information.

"I had a message from my ex. It said that . . ." she paused, "a man was after me because he thinks I took money from him."

Jake glanced at her, and she averted her eyes. He wasn't sure if it was in embarrassment or out of fear of his reaction.

Turning his eyes back to the road, he asked, "Who's the man?"

She had a flair for the expensive, but stealing money didn't fit what he'd seen of her.

Unless you're blinded by her pretty face.

He pushed that thought away as she spoke.

"Marco Soldano. He's rumored to be a crime boss in Chicago. I defended him in an extortion case last year. That's what I do," she explained. "I'm a lawyer. So is my ex. We

worked for the same firm. I think Trevor—my ex—led Marco to believe I took the money."

"Why would he do that?" Things hadn't ended well with Diana, but he couldn't imagine her ever trying to pin a crime on him.

What kind of person does that?

"Because he's a slimeball, apparently." Blair's voice dripped with self-loathing. "Look, I asked the same question, but essentially, we broke up, and I left town immediately. I think he used that to his advantage and placed the blame on me. He didn't call to warn me. He wanted me to answer." She shook her head and explained, "It was a company phone. They're issued to all the junior partners, and the firm tracks them. I destroyed it when I realized, but it's possible they already know I was at the bed and breakfast."

"Okay." He'd always considered himself a good judge of character, but he did wonder if his attraction for Blair was clouding that judgment.

Shaking off the thought, Jake told her what he'd found out, "There was a man that left the diner right after you. He definitely could have followed you on foot. He came back in under half an hour and drove away in the Mercedes you saw in the parking lot."

When he glanced over to gauge her reaction, she'd shut her eyes. "How do you know that?"

"My brother's on the police force. We watched the security tape."

"Of course he is," she muttered without opening her eyes.

It made him wonder if she was trying to shut out the situation or just him.

Hopefully, the situation.

Frowning over the other possibility, he turned his mind to her predicament, pondering it as they drove the rest of the way in silence. City woman or not, she was in trouble, and he couldn't leave her to fend for herself.

CHAPTER 5

Blair

"We're here," Jake announced.

Blair opened her eyes, surprised to find the very modern—very large—ranch home sprawled in front of her. The whole front side of the house seemed to be made of windows. Lights shone on the timber-framed portico, and stone retaining walls added to the masculine air. They were artfully constructed to blend in with the landscaping.

"Oh," she murmured. This was not at all what she'd expected from the man wearing worn jeans and driving a dirty pickup.

Staring at the mix of wood and stone, she wondered what it would look like in the sunshine. Compared to the one-bedroom apartment she'd shared with Trevor, it was a mansion. And that was saying something because they'd lived in a luxury apartment in Chicago's River North neighborhood.

"It's better in the daylight." Jake grinned at her.

She believed him. Clearly, there was more to Jake Redland than met the eye.

He grabbed her luggage, and she followed him inside. The interior was even more impressive. Warm hardwood floors gleamed against the cool colors on the walls. Modern furniture in neutral shades complemented the exposed ceiling beams and brass light fixtures. The house was sleek yet comfortable. It smelled faintly of fresh grass, which she found oddly pleasant.

Jake led her into the living room. "Have a seat," he offered. "I'm going to get a drink. Would you like one?"

"Sure." She settled onto a leather settee, thinking she could use a strong drink. Something to dull the pain of the headache that had formed between her eyes from worry and stress.

Jake came back with two beers. Not her first choice, but she accepted out of politeness.

"Do you have family you need to call, someone who can help you?" Jake asked as he perched on an ottoman across from her.

She looked at him sharply. "Do you think I would have called you if I did?"

Jake flinched as though she'd physically struck him and lowered the beer he'd been about to take a sip out of.

Watching him, she felt like a monster.

Harsh, Blair.

Although she was scared and angry, he didn't deserve to have it taken out on him.

She took a calming breath. "I'm sorry. That was

uncalled for." When he didn't say anything, she explained, "I only have my mother, and we're not very close. She won't miss me since we hardly talk, and I don't think bringing her into this is wise. I don't need to worry about Marco going after her . . . even if she isn't winning any trophies for Mother of the Year," she added, unable to hide the sarcasm in her voice.

"Look, Blair, you can stay here as long as you want."

She gave a grateful nod, glad he didn't push her on her family any further.

"I'm going to call Dillon, my brother who's the cop," Jake clarified, "and tell him everything you told me. If a crime boss is after you, the police need to know."

"You never asked me if I took it." The words flew out of her mouth before she could stop them.

His look told her she'd surprised him with her bold remark. "No, I didn't. I know you didn't steal anything."

It was her turn to look taken aback, surprised by his frankness. "Thank you," she told him quietly.

She wasn't used to someone blindly trusting her. But *Jake does*, she realized. They barely knew each other, and he was willing to take her at her word. It was a refreshing change and one she wasn't altogether comfortable with.

"I'll show you to the guest room."

When he rose, she set her beer down and followed. Exhaustion was starting to make her eyelids droop.

He led her down the hall, stopping at the open door to a bedroom. When she turned to thank him, he caught her hand.

Unsure what he was doing, she looked at him with questioning eyes. His gaze dropped to her lips, and she knew what he intended. He brought his eyes back to hers, begging for permission.

Her pulse raced, but she nodded ever so slightly. Jake tugged her closer; she could feel the heat radiating off his body. When he lowered his head and placed his lips on hers, her breath caught in her chest. It was gentle at first, but as he caressed her bottom lip with his tongue, she wanted more. So, she opened her mouth to let him in.

She wasn't prepared for the effect that had on Jake. He pulled her up hard against his length and devoured her. She stiffened, barely able to ride the wave of heat that crashed into her.

He must have sensed her hesitation because he—thankfully—ended the kiss.

"Goodnight, Blair." With a final searing look, he left her there.

She stared after him, too shocked to reply. Her hand involuntarily rose to her lips.

What was *that?*

She'd never been kissed like that before. Kissing Trevor was nice and even exciting at first, but it had never made her feel like she was on fire. The flames had nearly knocked her off her feet.

She'd been shocked, yes, but she'd wanted to devour him the same way he was devouring her. Not only that, but she'd wanted more than his mouth on hers.

What am I doing?

She shook herself, glad he'd left. No matter what her

body wanted, she wasn't ready to take that kiss any further. She barely knew the man, and if her relationship with Trevor had taught her anything, she'd been right to be wary of men and what they promised. She'd wasted five years of her life on one already.

No, she needed to keep her defenses carefully in place because Jake was coming at them like a battering ram whether she wanted him to or not.

Yawning, she had barely enough energy to take off her clothes and climb under the covers before she fell asleep.

* * * *

Jake

Jake tossed and turned, struggling for sleep. He'd informed Dillon of what Blair had told him about Soldano. After talking it through with his brother, he realized someone who knew Whiteford Farm had to have been involved with the silver Mercedes. The car wasn't local, and no one not local would know about the road Blair had been on—unless somebody told them.

He trusted the people of Rolling Brook. The town was small, and he had no enemies there. Only one man had the plans for Whiteford that hated his guts.

Chase Sinclair—the bastard.

It wouldn't surprise Jake if he was involved in this. He'd as good as declared he would do whatever it took to develop Whiteford. Jake would run it by Dillon tomorrow so he could question the snake.

"Dammit!" Jake punched his pillow. He was fully

involved now.

He'd let Blair in. All it had taken to crush his resolve was a sob story about her family. He'd sensed her relationship with her mother pained her. Though he'd wanted to pry about her father, he'd had no right. Not everyone was as lucky as him. He knew that.

His family was close, and he still had both of his parents. They were getting up there in age, but they never showed it. Hell, Jake had practically had to force his dad to retire last year and let him take over the farm. The man still woke up before sunrise on occasion and wandered down to the milking parlor.

A smile softened his face as he thought of his father. Brock Redland was a man who loved his animals like he loved his family. There had been so much love from both his parents growing up. That love had been a bear hug or a smack on the ass when they needed it, but it was love.

He'd never not be grateful for that. His heart went out to Blair, knowing her experience had been a bit different. He'd help her however he could, and if Sinclair had anything to do with this, Jake had a stake in the fight, too.

He groaned. Not only was he on edge about someone being after Blair, but he couldn't get thoughts of kissing her again out of his head.

He'd planned to leave her at the door to the guestroom, but as she'd brushed past him, her scent enveloped him. It was like honey and wildflowers, and he'd thought, why the hell not?

When she'd opened those plump pink lips for him, the

taste of her had driven him wild. He'd wanted to take her right there, up against the door. If she hadn't resisted, hell, he would have. Jake groaned again and wondered if he'd get any sleep tonight.

* * * *

Colt

The man from the diner watched as the lights in the sprawling ranch house turned off. He'd followed the woman here.

Waiting, he wondered at her relationship with the farmer.

Was he involved?

From the looks of his house, the man hardly needed that kind of money.

Well, not my problem.

Mr. Soldano would figure that out. Colt's job was to watch and wait for an opportunity to grab the woman. So that's what he'd do.

He had to admire her guts and her looks. She was a certified knockout. He'd have thought she'd be better at hiding, though, if she was going to steal five million dollars and expect to get away with it. But he couldn't complain about her making his job easier.

Colt grinned. Maybe he'd get to play with her a little. Thinking about it, he tested the edge of his switchblade with his thumb. Scaring them was half the fun. He'd come a little too close with that earlier, though.

Remembering, he shook his head.

Who doesn't move when a car comes barreling at them?

That had been a close one, and it would've been his head on the line if she'd been killed before they found out where the money was.

Chuckling now, he guessed the farmer was good for something. Too bad he'd probably have to kill him. Business was business, after all.

CHAPTER 6

Jake

Jake heard Blair screaming and launched himself out of bed. He threw on his jeans and grabbed the 20-gauge shotgun he kept propped in the corner by the door.

Rushing to the guestroom, he found her sitting up in bed, her breathing coming in rapid bursts.

Her eyes grew wide at the sight of him, then she shrieked and tried to scramble away.

Seeing no threat, he lowered the gun and slowly raised his hands to show Blair they were empty.

She was as scared as a prized filly who'd just seen a snake, and he knew he needed to appear non-threatening to calm her down.

"It's all right, Blair," he told her softly. "I'm not going to hurt you. I heard screaming and thought you were in trouble."

Her eyes were still wild when they met his, searching. As her gaze took everything in, he hoped she saw he had no intention of hurting her.

When she remained silent, he tried again. "Are you all right? Can you tell me what happened?"

Because he was watching her closely, he saw the change in her expression as the fear ebbed and the anger flowed in. She was about to unleash on him.

"I had a nightmare!" she yelled. "What are you doing charging in here and pointing that monstrosity at me?" Her half-naked body shook with rage as she climbed from the bed to confront him. "You scared me half to death! What's wrong with you?" She pushed against his chest, but the shove didn't even make him budge.

He was trying really hard not to laugh at her. She was livid and coming at him dressed in only a tank top and underwear. It clung to her slim figure. With her hair attractively mussed from sleep, his blood started to simmer. Laughing would only make the situation worse, but he thought she was damn cute when she was mad.

"Are you smiling at me? You think this is funny!" Blair screeched, and Jake lost the battle. His laughter came out in loud guffaws.

She stared at him, but he couldn't contain his mirth.

"Someone is after me, and you're *laughing*."

She'd barely breathed the statement, but it was enough to shock him out of his amusement. He stopped immediately.

"You're right. I'm sorry." He tried to look as genuinely apologetic as he felt and hoped she would forgive him. "Do you want to tell me about it?" he coaxed.

When she only stared, he prompted, "Your

nightmare?"

Something like fear flickered in her gaze before she sighed and sat back on the bed. "Marco's men were chasing me, and I, I got shot." Her hand instinctively covered her stomach. Anger crept back into her gaze as she stared him down.

He winced and ran his hand through his hair. He felt like a jerk. His barging in with a gun was so much worse after hearing that. "I'm sorry," he repeated. "Really. I didn't mean to scare you."

"I know," she finally relented.

Jake moved to sit beside her on the bed. She raised her eyes to look at him and what he saw in them destroyed him. Drawn in by her gaze, he forgot what he was going to tell her. Before he knew what he was doing, he kissed her. Slowly, softly.

His hands reached up to frame her face, lifting the hair off her neck. It was soft as silk; he wrapped a hand in it and held on, lost in her mouth, teasing with his tongue.

When he nipped at her lips, she opened for him. Again, it was like someone lit a fire in his blood, and he lost control. She tasted of honey, and it was both sweet and spicy.

He claimed her mouth with his tongue and pulled her tight to his chest. He was desperate to feel her skin on his. Thinking about it, his hand in her hair tightened, and she cried out.

"Stop! Jake, stop," Blair pleaded. She pushed against his chest, and he released her.

Her breathing was ragged, and he realized she was

afraid. He silently cursed himself for scaring her again.

She scooted away. "I can't, Jake. I'm sorry."

"You don't have to apologize," he assured her. As he rose to go, he said, "I'll let you get some sleep."

Blair stopped him before he reached the door. "Jake, wait. It's not that I don't want to. I just, I . . ." Her arms flailed about helplessly as though she struggled to find the right words. "Ugh! I'm no good at this," she complained.

A bolt of shock turned his face into a picture of disbelief. "You mean you've never?" He gestured between them. "Are you—?"

"No! I'm not a virgin. I've, um, I've only ever been with my ex. And the way you make me feel, it's . . ., it scares me." Jake noticed a blush form on her cheeks at the admission.

"How do I make you feel?" he asked, wanting to reach for her again, but he stopped himself.

"Like I'm on fire." Both fear and desire swam in her eyes. "Like the flames are engulfing me, and you're the one holding the match."

His libido sparked at her words, but he'd have to keep a tighter rein on his appetite for her if he wanted things to go any further.

"You make me burn, too." His eyes darkened with his desire on the admission, but he picked up his gun. "Goodnight, Blair." He needed to leave before he did something they'd both regret.

"Goodnight, Jake." She hugged herself as she watched him walk away.

CHAPTER 7

Blair

The next morning, Blair woke bleary-eyed to stare at the bedside clock. It was six-thirty, the usual time she got up for work. With a groan, she shut her eyes. She wasn't ready to face Jake. The man had kept her up half the night. She hadn't been able to stop wondering whether she'd made the right choice in asking him to stop.

But, by God, the man is infuriating!

The way he'd barged into her room like that nearly scared her half to death. After having had the mother of all nightmares, she'd awoken and hadn't been sure she wasn't still in it as she'd stared at the unfamiliar surroundings of the guest bedroom.

In her dream, there had been gunfire all around her as she'd run for her life. Marco's thugs had chased her, and she'd been shot. Remembering the pain of it now, Blair rubbed at her stomach.

She'd barely had a chance to feel relieved at still being

whole when he'd barged into her room, bare-chested and waving a gun around. And then he'd had the nerve to laugh at her.

Oh, but I quickly forgave him for that, didn't I? She mocked herself.

Sure, he cared about her safety, and considering what she was up against, it was a good thing he knew how to use a gun. But all Jake had to do was touch her, and she caved completely. Well, not entirely. She *had* asked him to stop. But she hadn't really wanted him to.

She didn't understand it. The man moved her in a way she'd never felt before. There was electricity between them, and whenever he touched her, it caused a spark.

Last night, as he'd taken her hand, she'd felt it tingle while the warmth spread up her arm. Then, sitting next to him on the bed, she hadn't been able to ignore the heat coming off his body at such close range. Her breath had hitched when she'd noticed his jeans were unbuttoned. He had to have thrown them on quickly to come to her aid, and that realization had made her feel safe.

But that kiss.

Blair touched her lips as she replayed it. The way he'd kissed her had nearly made her lose herself. She wasn't used to relinquishing control, and with one kiss, he seemed to take it all from her.

What scared her was that she'd wanted him to.

Shaking herself out of her reverie, Blair yawned. She'd never been a morning person and had only one thought now—coffee. Pulling on her wrinkled silk robe from her luggage, she covered herself. Then she wandered in the direction of the living room, hoping she'd find the kitchen on the way.

Boy, did she. Blair stepped into her dream kitchen. Wall-to-wall white cabinets framed a hand-carved range hood set over a 36-inch gas stove with a pot filler. A center island with a marble top dominated the room and held the sink. At its counter, there was room for six.

When she noticed a coffee bar to the left of the island, she made a beeline for it. She needed caffeine. Her body was used to at least two cups to start the day, and she typically drank a couple more in the afternoon.

Jake had left her a note by the pot full of the dark brew. She poured a cup from the mug he'd left her on the counter and inhaled like a drug addict getting his fix, which she guessed she was. Caffeine was a potent drug for her.

Glancing at the paper, she chuckled. "Really?" she asked aloud in the quiet.

The note said he'd gone to milk the cows and would be back around eight. That gave her time to shower and figure out what to do next. She poured a second cup of coffee and carried it back to her room.

* * * *

Blair

By eight, Blair was much more awake. With the caffeine in her system, she realized she needed details about her situation, and one person had them—Trevor.

She had to call him back and find out what he'd gotten

her into if she had any hope of getting out of it.

With her third cup of coffee in hand, she wandered out to the portico to wait for Jake. She looked out over the softly rolling hills and breathed in deep.

There's that fresh air again.

She inhaled greedily, wondering how she'd been content to live in the pollution of the city for so long. Being in the country still reminded her of her childhood. She could easily picture her grandmother's farmhouse amid the rolling hills here.

The thought made her wonder about Jake's farm. His property had to be pretty large because she didn't see any outbuildings nearby. In fact, nothing—no animals and no machinery—suggested this even was a farm.

Pondering where they might be, Blair glanced toward the road she'd traveled in on. She thought she saw sunlight glinting off of something beneath the trees, but she was distracted by a sound behind her. Spinning, she stared.

Jake rode toward her on the largest horse she'd ever seen.

Well, she hadn't seen a lot of horses, at least not in person, but this one looked huge. It had to stand over one and half times her height, but Jake sat in the saddle as though born to.

The way he confidently drove the gelding and stopped it right next to her made her think he must have grown up riding.

She hid her nervousness behind a sip of coffee, hoping things wouldn't be awkward between them after last night.

He hopped down and tied the reins around a porch post. "Mornin'." Though his expression was reserved, it wasn't hostile.

She breathed a sigh of relief. When she examined his face more closely, she noticed he looked tired. Offering him her coffee, she smiled and said, "Hi."

"Thanks." He took the mug and drank deeply.

"Curious, is this a normal day for you? Get up, feed cows, and ride horses?"

He smiled at the teasing in her voice. "Sometimes," he retorted. "But sometimes not. I have a good team here. Jim usually takes care of the cattle, but he called in sick. So"—Jake shrugged—"I had to milk the cows. The horse was a quicker way to get back here. I'd told you eight."

"Where *are* all the cows and horses?" she asked, genuinely interested in his farm.

"Whiteford's pretty big. We've got 10,000 acres here. The dairy barn and horse stables are a couple miles that way." Jake pointed in the direction he'd come from.

"Wow." It was all she managed to get out. *10,000 acres!*

His expression darkened with a scowl. "The size is one of the reasons I've had trouble with a developer out of Chicago. He wants to buy up most of it and turn it into a full-scale golf community."

He kicked at the ground with his boots and added, "I actually wanted to tell you about that. After talking with Dillon last night, I realized the developer might be working with your crime boss. At least, it's likely Sinclair fed him information about my property."

Her confusion must have shown on her face because he explained, "That road you were on yesterday? Only someone familiar with the area would know how to access it from the direction the Mercedes came from, and he's the only person I know who has it in for me."

Blair exhaled. "Okay, well, that's good, right? At least we have another lead to follow."

"Yeah, I was going to call Dillon about it this morning."

"Okay, this is good. It feels like we're doing something." She nodded to herself as some of the stress knots in her stomach came untied. "I was going to ask to use your phone, or if you could drive me into town to get a new one, I'd appreciate it. I need to talk to Trevor and find out what's really going on."

"I don't know, Blair. Do you think that's a good idea?" He scratched at the stubble on his cheek. Somehow, the little bit of dark scruff made him even more attractive. "If he's framing you for this, wouldn't it be best to lay low? Get the cops in Chicago working on it?"

"And tell them what, exactly?" she challenged, shaking the lust from her brain. "That I'm being chased by a man who has no criminal record—thanks to me—because he thinks I stole money from him? I'm sure that doesn't sound suspect at all." Her voice dripped with sarcasm. "Look, Jake, I need to find out what money it is I supposedly stole. I don't even know how much he thinks I took from him," she huffed and crossed her arms.

"Okay, but we talk to Dillon first. If we're going to call Trevor, I want him there for it," Jake insisted, then drained the cup of coffee.

She wanted to argue that it was her choice, her problem, and she didn't have to do it his way. But that was only her pride talking. She really needed his help, and if this developer of his was involved, their fates were entwined.

"Fine." She agreed, accepting the mug he held out for her.

"Give me a few minutes to take care of the horse," Jake told her as he untied the reins.

She nodded but wanted this nightmare over with as soon as possible.

* * * *

Jake

Jake walked Dusty to the stables and wished for more coffee. He'd been grateful for the cup Blair offered him, but he needed about a gallon more. He'd hardly slept.

Thoughts of her had consumed him, making him anything but appreciative of the five o'clock call that roused him from a very . . . stimulating dream about her.

Jake shook his head. A cold shower had been a necessary shock to his system, but after seeing her fresh as morning dew, standing on his porch with that sweetly hesitant smile, he felt that spark of desire again. It was a slow burn that he couldn't put out.

Not that he wanted to. No, what he wanted was to throw more kindling on it and watch it blaze.

A groan shook his throat. *But I need Blair to want that,*

too.

CHAPTER 8

Blair

When Jake turned the truck onto the main road, Blair thought she saw a flash of silver in the opposite direction. She strained to see, but nothing appeared. Shaking it off, she chalked it up to being paranoid as they drove to the police station in town.

When they parked, she noticed a police officer leaning against the faded stucco exterior of the Art Moderne building. The station was larger than she'd expected, considering the size of the town. She'd thought there would be only a sheriff or deputy, but the building in front of her boasted fifteen parking spots, five of which were filled with police cruisers. It looked large enough to house at least twenty officers. This fact helped settle some of the worry churning her stomach. She felt better about involving a police force that was large enough to actually help.

Jake turned the truck off, and Blair glanced at the cop

in front of the building again. He *had* to be Jake's brother.

Geez, what is it with this family?

Their parents must have rigged the gene pool lottery. Dillon was as good-looking as Jake. Possibly even more so if you went in for the military type. His dark hair was cropped short, making the blue of his eyes that much more prominent. Dillon looked a couple of inches shorter than Jake and trimmer, but he had wiry muscles beneath his crisp uniform shirt.

Noticing Jake was already rounding the hood, Blair hopped out of the pickup before he had a chance to open the door for her. Thankfully, he didn't comment on the move.

"Dill, this is Blair O'Rourke." Jake introduced her when they reached the cop. "Blair, my brother, Lieutenant Redland."

Dillon smiled and reached out his hand for a shake. "Nice to meet you, Miss O'Rourke, though I'm sorry about the circumstances."

"It's just Blair, please." She shook his hand, and no tingling sensation shot up her arm. The lack of reaction relieved her. Though handsome, he didn't affect her like Jake did.

Glancing sideways at him, she was surprised to see a quickly hidden stab of jealousy flare in his eyes.

Without commenting on Jake's reaction, she told Dillon, "Nice to meet you as well. I understand Jake's told you what's going on."

"Yes. Let's go inside, and we can discuss it further."

Dillon led them through a maze of cubicles into a

cramped office with a desk piled with papers. The metal filing cabinet in the corner stood open, and files jutted out at odd angles. Blair guessed organization wasn't Dillon's strong suit.

Noticing her examination, he shrugged. "I'm sorry about the disarray. I never was very good at keeping things tidy."

Jake snorted at that, laughing at an inside joke, she was sure.

Dillon gestured to the chairs in front of his desk. At least those were clear of papers. "Have a seat."

After they sat, Blair began, "I want to call Trevor. We need more information."

"I don't think it's a good idea." She glared at Jake's interjection.

Dillon scratched his chin. "Well, right now, we don't have a lot to go on. If we could get him talking, maybe pull more information out of him . . ."

She nodded in triumph. "Exactly. How do you want to do this?"

"You'll put it on speaker. Try to make nice, get him to open up. If Trevor's framing you, we need to know why."

Jake clenched his fists as she dialed. She knew he thought this would put her in more danger, but she had to start somewhere if she wanted out of this mess.

They waited while it rang and rang. Then, the operator recording informed them the number was no longer in service.

What? Trevor always had his phone on him. He'd never disconnect it. Unless he got fired, but that seemed unlikely.

"Well, that was a dead end," she stewed.

"That's interesting," Dillon said at the same time.

"What, why?" Jake asked.

"Well, if Trevor's trying to pin the blame on Blair, it's probable he stole the money himself. And if he was going to skip out with it, disconnecting the phone would be his first move. I think it's time we talked to Chicago. See if they can send someone to check up on him. Find out if he really is gone."

"Oh." Blair digested that. "Thank you."

"In the meantime, we're going to send a cruiser out to the farm. If they're after you, a show of force could be a deterrent."

She sighed. It was unbelievable. *This* was her life now—crime bosses and police cruisers.

Jake nodded. "Thanks, brother. Let us know what you find out about Trevor. And look into Sinclair like we talked about. What if there's a connection between him and Soldano? The man's business has always seemed shady." When Jake stood to go, Blair followed.

Dillon squeezed Jake's shoulder in a show of brotherly affection. "Stay alert."

He smiled in response. "Always." Then, he took her hand, which had Dillon raising an eyebrow at the easy gesture.

She chose not to bring any more attention to it by commenting on it. Instead, she thanked Dillon, and they found their way to the exit.

A pleasant warmth radiated out from where Jake's

rough palm clasped hers. She wasn't sure why he'd taken her hand, but she didn't mind the contact.

It kept her calm when she wasn't sure what to do next. She hoped Dillon would be able to work with the Chicago police to find Trevor soon because she needed to know what she was up against.

* * * *

Colt

So, they went to the cops.

Colt sneered as he watched the pickup drive away from the station. He'd have to call the boss and let him know. See if Mr. Soldano wanted him to proceed any differently. With the cops involved . . . well, he'd be fine with speeding things up.

Colt checked the bullets in his Colt 45. He'd gotten the nickname for a reason, after all. It was his finisher.

No matter how much he played with his knife, the final blow was always a round from his 45, right between the eyes.

Smiling at the thought, Colt trailed the woman and dialed his boss.

CHAPTER 9

Blair

After leaving the station, Jake drove her to the local electronics store for a replacement cell phone, but any hope Blair had of getting a new iPhone fizzled when he pulled into a parking spot in front of the 1930s brick storefront.

She sighed and turned to Jake. "Is this our only option?"

Not only did the exterior look old, but the appliances she saw in the window were barely from this decade.

He frowned at her question. "It's the only option in town. There's a Wal-Mart a few miles out, but, hey, we're already here." He nudged her shoulder and climbed out of the truck.

Guess I'm in for more of the small-town experience.

When she opened her door, Jake was there, waiting to help her out of the cab.

"I realize I'm short, but I *can* manage this by myself."

He smiled. "I know that, but I was raised to be chivalrous. What would my mother think if she saw me get out without offering you my arm?"

Blair snorted. "Please! I'm sure your mother wouldn't care one way or the other."

Though she wanted to be indignant, she had to smile at his stubborn gallantry. After a shake of her head, she reached out for his hand, but Jake grabbed her around the waist instead.

He set her down gently and held on. Mirth shone in his eyes as he stared down at her, making Blair grin despite herself. The longer he held her, though, the more aware she became of the heat coming off his body.

As she continued to stare into his eyes, something shifted, and for a moment, she thought he would kiss her again.

Her breath caught in her throat with anticipation, but he only grinned and released her.

"If you don't believe me, you can ask her yourself. She's inside." He hooked his thumb in the direction of the electronics store, giving her a moment of panic.

Is he serious?

She scanned the store. There was a woman who looked to be the right age. Blair swallowed. She was going to meet his mother, just like that.

"Oh, right. Uh-huh. I'll . . . do that." She cleared her throat and gestured for him to lead the way.

When he laughed, she had to shake her head. *Honestly, the man could find anything funny.*

She wished she had his sense of humor. Her palms

were sweating at the thought of—

"Jake, wait! What do we tell her?" She grabbed his arm to stop him. "I don't want her to know what's going on. If she knows, she could be in danger." Now, the thought of meeting his mother was causing her a whole new level of anxiety.

His smile disappeared. "You're right." He paused and ran a hand through his mane of shaggy dark hair. "I guess we could tell her we've been dating and you came to stay for a few days."

"What?" Blair shrieked. "Why does she need to know I'm staying with you? Can't we just say we met at the diner or something, and you offered to show me where to get a new phone when I mentioned I lost mine?"

"Trust me, she already knows you're staying at the farm." He shrugged as though it was no big deal.

Blair, on the other hand, tried not to melt from embarrassment. "What? How would she know that?"

"My guess," Jake started, "probably Janet. I'm sure she saw you leave with me last night. It's a small town. People talk."

That didn't make her feel any better. "If the whole town knows, then it won't be hard for Marco's men to find me."

"No. You don't have to worry about that. Look, something else this town has is loyalty. People won't talk to just anybody."

That didn't wholly reassure her, but she didn't know what other choice she had.

Groaning, she pulled at her hair and tangled the long blonde waves. "Great! We'll go with your plan then," she said, voice loaded with sarcasm. She didn't like the idea of lying to Jake's mother about their relationship, but she didn't see another option.

He grabbed her hand; she wasn't sure if it was part of the ruse or if he just wanted to hold it. She surprised herself by hoping it was the latter.

His palm was huge compared to hers, but she loved the feel of it. With his grip closed around hers, she felt safe. Right now, she needed that more than she knew.

When he opened the door to the store, she took a deep, calming breath. They stepped inside to the tinkling of a tiny bell hanging above the door. At the sound, the woman she'd seen and the older gentleman behind the counter turned to look at them.

"Jake!" The woman practically squealed.

She looked to be in her late fifties at best guess, but she'd clearly aged well. There were a few wrinkles on her lightly tanned skin, though not as many as Blair's own mother tried to conceal, and she was only fifty-two.

The woman's short bob of brunette hair swung as she rushed over to meet them. Jake grabbed her in a half-hug, and Blair smiled at the genuine affection on the woman's face. It was soft with high round cheeks and, she realized, Jake's nose. He'd clearly gotten that from his mother. Looking at the two of them together, she had to smile. There was a lot of love there.

"This is so great running into you. I wanted to come over to the farm and meet your . . . friend." His mother smiled, a delighted twinkle lighting her eyes that surprised Blair. At least she didn't seem upset that she was staying at Jake's. "But I didn't want to intrude."

Blair looked at Jake with expectant eyes until she realized he was trying to contain a laugh. Since he was still holding her hand, she dug her nails into his palm.

"Jake," she said as sweetly as she could through clenched teeth, "aren't you going to introduce me?"

He coughed, and she wanted to elbow him, but he wasn't close enough for her to do it surreptitiously.

"Are you all right, dear?" his mother asked.

Thankfully, he cleared his throat and got himself under control. "Yes, ah, just a tickle in my throat. It's good to see you, too, Mom. This is my girlfriend, Blair. Blair"—he turned to her, and she glared at the laughter shining in his eyes—"this is my mom, Sandra."

"Oh, call me Sandy, please. Everyone does."

Blair reached out to shake her hand, and Sandy crushed her in a hug. She was too surprised to hug back at first, but his mom held on. After several long seconds, she patted Sandy's back, and the woman released her.

"It's so great to meet you. When I heard you were staying at the farm, I . . . well, never mind that." She waved her hand as if shooing away what she was going to say. "How long have you been dating? Jake has said not a word, the rascal."

Sandy lightheartedly swatted him on the arm. "Are you from Chicago? Is that where you two met? Oh! I have so many questions, but I can see this is too much. Yes, yes. We'll get together and have a chat. Jake"—she turned to her son, who chuckled at her 'so many questions' comment—"you two have to come to dinner on Sunday night."

Blair's smile became a little wicked when she looked at Jake.

Not chuckling now, are you?

She enjoyed watching him squirm to get out of this one.

"Oh, yeah, maybe, Mom. We'll let you know. Blair might have to be back in the city by then."

"Oh, but . . ." Sandy looked so crestfallen that Blair couldn't help it; she lied.

"We'll be there, Mrs. Redland. I promise."

A delighted smile spread across his mother's face. "Sandy, please. That's wonderful! Oh, I can't wait. I'll let you do what you came in for then. And I'll see you both"— she gave them each a hug again—"on Sunday. Seven o'clock."

"Mrs. Redland!" The man behind the counter called out as Sandy opened the door to the store.

She turned around with a puzzled look on her face.

"Mr. Redland's phone." The man held up a small smartphone, and she walked over to retrieve it.

"Oh! Gosh, I forgot all about it when you two came in. Thanks, Franklin." She turned to Jake to explain, "Your father dropped it again, and we had to get the screen fixed." Sandy shook her head. "The man is horrible on phones."

Jake nodded. "Yep, sounds like Dad. Tell him I said 'hello'." He bent down and gave her a kiss on the cheek. "Love you, Mom."

Sandy smiled. "Love you, too. See you both on

Sunday." With that, she waved and left.

As the bell jingled over the door, Blair had to fight the urge to run after Sandy and tell her the truth.

Why did she say that?

They couldn't go to his parents' house for dinner this weekend. Bad men were hunting her!

Jake must have sensed her anxiety because he grabbed her hand again and squeezed it. When he pulled her away from the door, they walked to the counter hand in hand.

"Hiya, Franklin. Blair needs a new cell phone. What do you got?"

She tried to focus on the man behind the counter. He was tall and lanky with a fuzzy gray beard and a balding head. His expression was hardly what she'd call friendly as he pointed to the case that housed the phones.

She knew a new one was vital if she was going to get out of this mess. Bending over the case to look at the options, she lost track of her thoughts. Her mind wasn't focused on the contents.

Sunday won't be a problem.

She would be out of there by then, and Jake could say they broke up over . . . *something.* She was sure he'd find a reason, and there would be no harm, no foul. His mother would be fine—disappointed, but fine.

Blair was nodding at herself until Franklin interrupted her thoughts. "What kind are ya looking for, miss?"

"Kind?"

"Of cell phone."

She realized she must seem dense because Franklin

stared at her as if she needed him to elaborate.

"Oh." She mentally shook herself and focused on the task at hand. "Do you have iPhones?"

Surprisingly, he answered in the affirmative. "Got a brand new one if you want it."

She'd had a newer model than the one he offered, but she figured at least it was an iPhone. With everything else going on, she didn't want to try to figure out a new operating system.

"I'll take it. Thank you." She tried to smile at him, but the man ignored her and moved to get the phone.

"Not very talkative, is he?" she commented to Jake.

He shrugged. "Franklin's a little curmudgeonly, sure, but he knows electronics."

"Jake," Blair started. She wanted to tell him she was sorry she lied to his mother, but she found herself tripping over the words. "I like your mom," she managed instead. Sandy was warm and open, whereas her own mother was cold and aloof.

He smiled at that. "Most people do. She's great. A whirlwind of energy, but you learn to go along with it, and then it's not so—"

When he paused, she supplied "exhausting" with a smile.

Jake chuckled. "Yeah, I guess it could be."

"I probably won't be here on Sunday." She lowered her voice. "You'll have to make something up. Tell them we broke up. I'm sorry, but I just couldn't disappoint her."

He frowned at her, about to say something, but Franklin interrupted them.

"Here you are. All set up."

She took it from him, surprised at how quick he'd been. "Thank you."

After she paid for the phone, Jake reached for her hand again. Her chest warmed with pleasure. It hadn't been just for the ruse. He did actually want to hold her hand.

She smiled as they left the electronics store, and no thoughts of Trevor or what he'd gotten her into crossed her mind.

CHAPTER 10

Jake

Blair fidgeted in the seat beside him, toying with the buttons on the new phone they'd picked up for her. He figured she wasn't happy waiting for information; he didn't like sitting around waiting for someone to come after her, either.

The thought of anyone trying to hurt her made his blood boil. He might've just met her, but he knew she didn't deserve that. What they needed was a distraction, and while he could think of a really good one, that option wasn't on the table.

At least, not right now.

Not to mention, he had another issue to handle since they'd lied to his mom. He didn't know what had come over Blair to agree to dinner like that, but he'd have to deal with the aftermath.

Unless she stays.

Jake sighed. He didn't have much hope of that, but

the more he thought about it, the more he wanted her to.

As he pulled up in front of the house, the sun hung heavy in the sky. It would start its descent soon. Watching the colors deepen on the horizon gave him an idea.

Once he'd parked, he shifted in his seat to see Blair. "Up for a walk?"

She seemed distracted when she met his gaze. "What?"

"I want to show you something." He reached into the back seat and snagged the blanket he always kept there. Without waiting for her to protest, he added, "Let's go."

Jake climbed out of the truck and rounded the hood to get Blair, who stepped down before he had a chance to assist her.

A smile touched her lips in triumph at beating him, then was gone with a sigh. "Where are we going?"

He grabbed her delicate palm, loving how soft her skin felt held within his rough hand. "Up that hill." He nodded with his head, and her eyes widened a little.

"That's a big hill."

His house sat in a valley, but at the top of the far hill, the view of the property and the setting sun would be glorious.

He couldn't help but chuckle at her comment. "I'll carry you if you get tired."

She arched a blonde eyebrow at him. "You're hilarious."

With a smile, he tugged her along as they started the trek. The walk was only about a mile, but it was mostly on an incline. It took them long enough to reach the top of the hill for the sun to start setting by the time they made it.

Jake spread the blanket over the fresh grass while Blair caught her breath. She'd kept up with him despite her much shorter limbs, shooting him dirty looks whenever he'd started to offer to slow down.

With a smile, he sat on the cloth and gestured for her to join him. You could see his parents' home from the crest of the hill. They still lived on the property in the house he'd grown up in. When it came time for him to take over the farm, he hadn't wanted to deprive them of that. So he'd had his own house built—several miles away. He loved his family, but he needed space, too. He pointed their home out to Blair.

It was little more than a speck from this distance, but she squinted with a scrunch of her nose. "Is that what you wanted to show me?"

He could swear he heard the wheels turning behind her pretty eyes.

Jake shook his head. "Turn your brain off and just look."

The sunset gleamed like a painting before them. The sky bled from pale purple to orange to pink as if someone had spilled watercolors across it. Floating within the mixture, the yellow ball of the sun created shadows that played over the green of the grass, darkening it from moss to emerald.

"It's beautiful here."

The note of awe in her voice filled Jake's chest with

pride. He glanced over at her with a smile.

The setting sun lit her face, highlighting the faint freckles across her skin. A bolt of desire zinged through him. He wanted to trace them with his tongue, testing the flavor of each one.

"Is this all part of the farm?" She waved her arms at the hills surrounding them.

"Yes." He couldn't stop staring at her.

Her hair glowed with red highlights in the retiring sun, and the gold flecks in her eyes sparkled with its shine. There was something so artless about her looks. It drew him in like nothing ever had before.

He sucked in a sharp breath and rasped out, "Can I kiss you?"

A blush filled her cheeks, highlighting the freckles there. He loved the way her skin flushed so easily. "I don't . . ." She nibbled on her bottom lip, deepening it to a deep ruby color. "I don't think that's a good idea."

Perhaps she was right, perhaps not. Instead of arguing about it, he shrugged it off with a smile. He could wait until she was ready. "How 'bout some dinner, then?"

"Dinner would be divine. I'm starving."

* * * *

Blair

"You don't cook?" Blair asked, wrinkling her nose at the contents of Jake's refrigerator.

She felt him come up behind her, caging her between the open door and the inside of the appliance as he leaned over her shoulder. His head hovered next to hers. So close if she turned her face, they'd be touching. She sucked in a sharp breath, reiterating why kissing him was *not* a good idea.

You're leaving soon.

You barely know him.

No sense getting attached.

His strong arm reached in and shuffled things around. "I eat at the diner most nights."

When his shoulder brushed hers, electricity flowed out from the spot, making her body buzz with nerves. Avoiding eye contact with him at all costs, she grabbed a carton of eggs, a half-eaten block of cheese, and the only green thing she could find—chives.

Turning with it all in her arms, she used it as a barrier to keep him at bay. "Excuse me."

Jake grinned down at her like he knew exactly what she was doing, but he at least stepped aside for her to pass.

Setting everything on the center island, she asked, "Do you have any potatoes?"

"Might." He disappeared while she started opening cabinets to find a mixing bowl.

When he returned, he tried to hand her two golden potatoes, but she motioned for him to wash them in the sink.

"Who taught you how to cook?" Jake asked as he rinsed the potato skins free of dirt.

Blair felt her mood flop when she thought about her past. Her father had always cooked, and after the divorce, she'd learned it was because her mother didn't know how.

"I taught myself," she told him in a quiet voice. She'd had to if she'd wanted anything more than a microwave meal for dinner.

"My mom tried to teach all of us, but it never really stuck for me." His sheepish smile made her laugh.

"I feel like that could've been intentional." She wouldn't put it past him, that's for sure.

"Where do you want these, chef?" He held up the cleaned potatoes.

She stopped searching for cooking utensils and shook her head at the moniker. She'd hardly call herself a chef. "On the counter is fine."

"Great, what next?" He started to advance on her, and she held up a hand.

If she was going to make them dinner, she needed distance. It helped keep her body in line because it tended to do things she wasn't comfortable with whenever he was near. "I need a cutting board, a knife, a skillet, a spatula, and a whisk."

Noting the smirk he didn't bother to hide as he turned away to do as she'd asked, she got the feeling he knew exactly how he affected her.

When he'd procured everything she needed, she got to work. Her stomach had already growled twice to let her know it was empty.

"So, what are we making?"

"We?" She stopped slicing the potatoes and arched a brow at him.

"Okay, *you*. What are *you* making?" He pulled out a

stool and sat at the counter to watch her.

She started whisking the eggs, explaining, "A Spanish omelet, though not a traditional one since we're adding cheese and using chives instead of onion."

He scratched at the stubble along his jaw, distracting her. She wanted to feel it for herself.

"Sounds fancy. I've never had one."

Blair forced all thoughts of his scruff from her head. "It's not. It's just potatoes and eggs, really."

"Would you like some wine?"

Her head snapped up from her task. His question surprised her. After last night, she'd figured him for a beer drinker. "Oh, yes, thank you." Maybe a glass would help settle some of the nerves, making her stomach jump whenever their eyes connected. What *was* that about?

"Be right back."

While she sipped her wine and focused on fixing dinner, Jake called Dillon to tell him about the run-in with their mother. If they were going to keep up the ruse of dating for Sandy's safety, then Dillon needed to know about it.

Jake clearly didn't care if she overheard their conversation because he made the call sitting five feet behind her. Still, propriety dictated she try not to listen in. When she heard him mention Trevor, though, her ears perked up.

"He's skipped town?" With a frown in her direction, he said, "Hold on. I'm going to put you on speaker for Blair."

She checked the omelet in the pan. It needed to cook for a few minutes before she flipped it, so she moved closer to Jake and the phone he'd laid on the counter.

Dillon's voice came through the speaker. "Trevor's gone. The Chicago police searched his apartment this afternoon. There's no trace of him. Blair, if you have any idea where he could have gone, let me know."

Her stomach twisted like marled yarn. Why would Trevor leave? What did it mean? After everything in the last twenty-four hours, her brain was spent, and she could think of nothing to help Dillon. "I'm sorry. I don't know."

Jake reached for her hand and gave it a squeeze. She met his gaze with a grateful nod. How did he seem to know what she needed before she knew herself?

"We'll call you if she thinks of anything." Jake took the phone off speaker, and she wandered back to the stove while they said goodbye.

Her mind kept going in circles; she tried to think of where Trevor might have gone. But the more she thought about it, the less she realized she'd truly known her ex. They'd spent five years together, but she'd never met his family. In fact, he'd never talked about them other than to mention they didn't get along. With her own melancholy past, she hadn't wanted to make him relive any painful memories, but it meant she'd never really gotten to understand him. How could she have thought she wanted to marry a man she barely even knew?

The question was made worse when she realized she'd met more of Jake's family and knew more about them than Trevor's. Especially since she'd only known the man for a matter of days.

When Jake's hands landed on her shoulders, she jumped and tensed. Until they started kneading the tension out of her neck. Her eyes closed on a moan. She forgot about the omelet, Trevor, the mess she was in. Nothing mattered but how good Jake's hands felt, massaging her.

"I think it might be burning."

"Hmm?"

"The omelet. It's smoking."

Her eyes flew open. "Oh, shoot!" She slid the skillet off the burner and grabbed the spatula to flip the omelet before all hope of saving dinner was lost.

It was definitely a little dark on one side, but they could cut away the worst pieces, she hoped. Staring at the charred eggs, she blushed in embarrassment. Afraid to meet Jake's gaze boring into her. Whenever he touched her, her brain stopped working.

Without looking at him, she gulped from her wine glass and said, "I think it'll still be edible."

"Good, because I'm beyond hungry."

Had his voice always sounded so gravelly? It sent a skitter of excitement racing across her skin. She snuck a glance at him out of the corner of her eye, and the stare leveled at her made her insides quiver and combust.

Holy moly. Something told her he wasn't talking about food. She looked away and swallowed hard.

What am I going to do about him?

CHAPTER 11

Jake

Jake forced himself out of bed at six a.m. after a restless night. At least Blair hadn't had another nightmare, but knowing she slept only a few walls away meant his dreams had been full of her.

He'd started the day with a cold shower and an extra cup of coffee. The caffeine had done its job, and he felt considerably more awake for their morning grocery run. One—according to Blair—that was much-needed if they wanted to eat something other than omelets.

He smiled, thinking of how she'd made them dinner last night. Even half burnt, the omelet had been one of the best things he'd ever tasted. She'd blushed when he'd told her that, then fled to her room, leaving him with clean-up duty. Not that he minded. He'd happily do the dishes if it meant she made more meals like that.

His heart thumped in his chest. That line of thinking was dangerous. He had no idea how many nights they'd even have together.

Trying not to dwell on the unknowns, Jake glanced over at her as he pulled onto the driveway. Tension seemed to vibrate off her. Maybe she was right, and acting on the attraction they both felt—because he knew she felt it too—*was* a bad idea.

Despite the caution his head demanded, he couldn't stop wanting her. At this rate, he feared he was setting himself up for another failed relationship. Just like Diana. Because no matter how Blair felt about him, she was from Chicago, and Whiteford Farm was about as far from city life as you could get.

Frustrated by his thoughts, Jake dragged his gaze away. They were still waiting for news, which meant they needed something to take their minds off it. As he put the truck in park, he had an idea that could serve as the distraction they both needed.

I wonder if she's ever ridden a horse.

He figured he could show Blair the farm via horseback in hopes a ride would help her relax. It usually helped him, so he thought it was worth a try. Then they could have a picnic by the lake.

He cut the ignition and asked, "How about a trail ride?"

"You mean, like on a horse?"

He nodded.

"I don't know how. I've never ridden a horse before."

He grinned, thinking about teaching her. "Well, it's never too late to learn."

"Okay. Why not?" She shrugged her shoulders.

After he hopped out of the cab, he headed for Blair's door. The fact she let him open it this time wasn't lost on him. He was even more delighted when she didn't bother refusing the hand he offered to help her step down.

In fact, he decided to hold onto her hand as he grabbed the grocery bag from the back seat.

He was doing that a lot lately—holding her hand. Good thing she didn't seem to mind.

* * * *

Blair

When they reached the stables, Jake let go of her hand, and Blair sighed. She'd relished the warmth that spread up her arm with the contact. It was both strange and exciting to feel this way. No man had ever had such an effect on her.

The more time she spent with Jake Redland, the more she wanted to get to know him better. He clearly loved his family and trusted his brother to help them resolve things. She also placed her trust in that. It was a new move for her and one she was trying not to dwell on. As a lawyer, she was a champion at arguing, even with herself.

Jake gestured her over to a stall where a pretty chestnut mare poked its head out.

"This is Molly. She's a gentle one. You shouldn't have any issues riding her," Jake assured Blair as he stroked Molly's head.

Unsure, she put her hand out, but he nodded at her

with a smile. The mare breathed on her palm, then nudged Blair's hand toward her head.

She laughed. "I guess Molly wants a pet." She patted the mare's face and was surprised to find the fur felt like human hair, though one that had been cropped close.

"I'm going to saddle her for you, then get my own mount."

He was quick and had both horses by the reins within ten minutes. Staring at the large animals, she gulped.

We're really doing this.

He ran through the basics with her before helping her lift herself onto the mare's back. He still held the reins, and she was grateful for that because she was having second thoughts.

This will be fun, right?

If she managed to stay on the thing and not get stomped by its giant hooves. Blair grimaced at the thought.

"This is a lot higher than it looked from the ground," she said, still wavering over her decision to do this.

"Oh, it's not that bad," he paused and searched her face. "Do you want to get down?"

She thought about it, but she wasn't a coward. Besides, she *would* like to see his farm.

How hard could it be?

"No, I'm doing this."

He handed her the reins and swung himself onto the back of a large bay gelding. They went through the basic motions again now that she was mounted.

Okay, she could do this. *Tap to go, pull to stop.*

Blair tapped her heels on the mare's sides, but nothing happened. Molly simply turned her head around and stared.

Thankfully, Jake didn't laugh at her. "Just give her a gentle squeeze with your legs—into her sides."

She tried again, following his instruction, and the horse moved forward. "I did it!" she spun around and declared.

As he caught up to her, she noticed his smile. "We'll start with a trot until you get comfortable enough to try a canter."

Blair nodded. That sounded reasonable, but she wasn't sure she would ever be ready for anything faster than a snail's pace.

* * * *

Jake

Blair had taken to riding with an innate and natural grace. Watching her sit the horse wasn't helping him tamp down the desire burning through his veins. In truth, he felt the opposite of relaxed.

"Oh, how pretty!" She pulled to a stop at the top of a small hill.

He halted his horse next to hers and drank in the radiance of her smile as she gazed down at the small lake on his property.

The noonday sun shone bright enough to cast the sky's reflection on the water's surface. Pale blue dotted with strips of white clouds floated serenely over the lake.

He'd planned to bring her here for a picnic, but there was something he wanted much more than food.

Swallowing down the need to taste her, he told her, "Let's walk the horses down, then we can unload our supplies."

She wore a puzzled look that scrunched the freckles across her nose. "What supplies?"

He chuckled as he hopped down and grabbed the reins for both animals. After the morning of exploring, they were probably ready for a drink and snack, too. "Lunch."

A dazzling smile lit her face. "We're going to have a picnic?"

Jake nodded, watching her eyes sparkle in the sun. When her feet came out of the stirrups, he moved to help her dismount.

"Swing your leg over, and I'll catch you."

She leaned her weight on the pommel and started to sling her leg across the mare's back. When her balance wobbled, he gripped her hips. "I've got you."

With both of Blair's legs on the same side, her tight little behind was at eye level. Jake gulped and lifted her off the horse. If he let her curves slide against him, well, he was only human.

He heard her sharp intake of breath at the contact and swallowed a groan. When she turned in his arms, his head automatically lowered. Her eyes were dark green pools, drowning him. He'd never wanted to kiss a woman so badly. Desire drummed its deafening beat in his pulse.

He couldn't look away, didn't want to. When her palms came up to rest on the tops of his arms while she stood on her tiptoes, his breath stuttered in his chest. *She* was going to kiss *him.*

When her mouth met his, liquid heat surged through their connection, suffusing him with its burning pleasure. He tried to hold himself back, but the longer her lips teased him, the more his blood pooled south. He lost himself in her taste, her scent. The birds chirping around their heads ceased to exist. All he could find was Blair.

Until his gelding bumped him, and the world around them came rushing back. After she pulled away, he watched her, breathing harder than the kiss warranted. Visions of taking her against the basswood tree behind her clouded his brain. He couldn't speak. Not yet.

A blush filled her cheeks, turning them a vibrant red. "Jake, I . . ."

Her gaze fell to his waist, and he knew she'd felt how much he wanted her. Her mouth opened as she met his gaze, but he didn't want to hear those two little words she was about to say.

He wouldn't apologize for wanting her, and he sure as hell didn't want her to be sorry she'd kissed him. The only thing he felt sorry about was that they hadn't finished what they'd started.

Turning away, he captured both horses' reins and started down the hill. "Let's have that picnic."

CHAPTER 12

Blair

She'd really done it now. Blair had to stop herself from chewing on a nail as she watched Jake set up things for their lunch. Her nerves had decided to camp out in her stomach, and she felt as jumpy as an exposed wire. One wrong move, and she'd set off sparks.

Since she'd kissed him, Jake had been uncharacteristically quiet. A heavy silence had settled between them. They'd been having a wonderful day until she ruined it.

I shouldn't have kissed him.

She tried to tell herself it was a mistake, but even now, watching him tend to the horses, she ached to do it again.

He wanted her. She'd seen it in his eyes and then felt the evidence of his desire when their bodies were pressed close. Remembering, she twisted her fingers in the grass below her seat, ripping it up in frustration. If she were going to throw caution to the wind, it had to be for more than just the physical.

But how could she tell him that?

He unrolled a plaid blanket, laying it around five feet from the water's edge. With a glance in her direction, he finally spoke. "You can sit on this if you'd like."

At this rate, grass stains on her jeans were the least of her worries. Still on edge, she rose, propping her hands on her hips. "Jake."

He leaned back on his heels, where he knelt on the blanket. "Yeah?"

Goodness. She'd faced down entire juries with less fear but needed to get this over with. Gulping, she wiped her sweaty palms on the sides of her pants. "I like you, but we just met. I can't, that is, I *won't* be pressured to jump into bed with you."

The muscle in his jaw worked as he clenched it. Then his chest heaved with an angry sigh before he gritted out. "You think I'm pressuring you?"

"Yes," her automatic reply felt wrong as it crossed her lips. She shook her head. "No. I just . . ." Trailing off, she blew out a breath. This hadn't exactly gone the way she'd imagined it would. Lowering her voice, she forced the words out, "You make me feel things—" His eyes were like molten glass stealing the words from her mind. She had to look away. "Even if I want to, Jake, it's too soon."

He didn't say anything, but the anger seeped from his expression.

Wanting him to accept her stance, she tried to explain, "Trevor and I were together for five years, but I don't think . . ." She trailed off, biting her lip while Jake waited for her to finish her thought. She used to be a lot better at arguing her case. He was making her unusually tongue-tied. "This sounds terrible, but I don't think I really knew him. The person I thought he was—" She shook her head, and a frown tugged at her lips. "Well, I was wrong."

Jake stood, approaching her slowly as if afraid she'd run. She tilted her head to meet his gaze when he was a foot away.

"I like you, too. And yes, I want you in my bed, but I'd never take you there, unwilling." The muscle in his jaw ticked as if the mere idea pissed him off. "You want slow? I'm fine with that."

The nerves bundled in her stomach started to ease. She gave him a tentative smile. "Thank you."

The fact that he was willing to go at her pace made her like him even more. When he offered his hand, she cautiously took it. Electricity still shot up her arm, but now she welcomed its zing.

"What's for lunch?"

* * * *

Colt

Colt watched the farmer and the woman from behind a copse of trees. Mr. Soldano wasn't pleased when he told him the cops were now involved. He'd ordered Colt to get rid of the farmer and grab the woman as soon as possible. The feds were already looking into the theft, meaning they might find more than Mr. Soldano wanted.

Colt wasn't sure who'd tipped them off, but he

wouldn't put it past the weasel boyfriend. Trevor never had the stomach for what they did.

He thought reaching out to him in the first place was a bad idea, but Mr. Soldano had wanted a powerful law firm on his side for scrapes like this one.

Colt checked his weapon again. It would do him no good at this range. Best to wait for the cover of darkness when he could get closer.

CHAPTER 13

Blair

They'd been riding around Whiteford Farm for hours, and Blair's backside was starting to feel it. She'd surprised herself by how much she enjoyed it. Once they'd begun to canter, she'd lost her fear and embraced the freedom she felt with the wind blowing through her hair and the animal flexing underneath her.

They traveled over a good portion of Jake's land. After they picnicked by the lake, he showed her fields where cattle grazed that he sold for beef, the pastures where the milk cows lazed in the sun, and a small retaining pond that looked ripe for fishing.

Now, she found herself staring at him. The man painted quite the picture on horseback. She smiled, noting how positively he belonged here. When he'd told her about the operations of the farm, she'd heard the pride in his voice, and she admired his connection to it. She'd certainly never had that in Chicago. She'd only ever known that sense of ownership and belonging when she'd visited her grandmother's farm as a child.

She'd told him about it as they rode, and he'd smiled as she recounted memories of feeding hogs and shearing sheep. Those memories had been the only times with her family that she could remember feeling loved and happy, and it had been nice to share them with someone who understood what they meant to her. Trevor had certainly never cared to hear about her childhood on her grandmother's farm.

With a sigh, she pushed thoughts of her ex-boyfriend away. Despite the situation hanging over her head, her road trip had garnered her the peace about the breakup she'd been searching for. The only thing that caused any pain now was how blind she'd been to the reality of their relationship.

"Last stop." Jake's announcement tugged her back into the present, leaving her past with Trevor in the dust kicked up by the horse's hooves, where it belonged.

They pulled the horses to a stop in front of a large white outbuilding. Dismounting, Jake slid open the large gray barn doors.

She gasped in delight at what she saw inside. This was a workshop. Half-finished pieces of furniture sat on tables, while tools she didn't recognize but assumed were for carpentry littered the workspace.

She inhaled the smell of fresh wood shavings. "You build furniture."

"Among other things," he told her with a smile.

Conscious of her sore backside, Blair carefully

dismounted from her horse and wandered through the rows of tables. Before she knew it, she found herself touching pieces in various stages of production.

"Oh!" She paused at a beautifully carved mahogany mantle. It looked to be nearly finished. The craftsmanship was familiar, and suddenly she knew. "You made the reception stand at the bed and breakfast."

"I did." He pointed at the mantel. "That piece is for one of the bedrooms there."

"It's beautiful work, Jake." She ran her hand along the delicate carvings.

"Thank you. I'm glad you think so." He didn't seem as uncomfortable with the praise as she would have been.

Her curiosity got the better of her, and she asked, "Is this a hobby, or do you do this full-time?"

"Somewhere in between, I think. I've done some large jobs like with the restoration of the bed and breakfast, but a lot of the pieces are gifts for family or furnishings for my home." He shrugged. "The farm is my full-time job. I've done less of this"—he waved his hand around the room—"since I took it over from my father last year."

No regret tinged his voice. Jake was comfortable doing both. She admired not only his skill but his dedication to his family. It was such a contrast to her own experiences with her parents.

She sighed inwardly. For too many years, she'd longed for that closeness but knew she'd never have it with her mother. After her parents divorced, she'd barely seen her father. The separation hadn't been amiable, and her mother had taken full custody. Then, her father had gotten sick, and Blair lost him to cancer at the tender age of ten.

Shaking off the melancholy her memories brought on, she forced a smile. "You're one interesting man, Jake Redland."

"You think so?" He winked at her, making her chuckle. If she wasn't careful, she could fall for him.

Following Jake back outside, her fingers touched pieces of his craft as they went. It was clear to her the man had a gift.

"It's getting dark. We should head back. Are you up for another canter?"

She didn't realize how late it had gotten. The sun was starting to set. The days were still short, spring having barely begun. "Absolutely." She grinned, impressed with her own prowess on horseback.

They mounted, and Blair kept pace with Jake as they made their way to the house. They were nearly there when a loud noise startled the horses. The animals reared, making her lose her grip on the reins.

A scream ripped from her throat when she felt herself slipping off the mare's back. She hit the ground with a thud, and her breath whooshed out.

Struggling to suck in air and sit up, Blair watched Jake get his gelding back on all fours and leap from the saddle.

More shots sounded, and the horses took off.

"Jake! Is that gunfire?" she shouted over the noise.

He didn't answer but grabbed her hand and pulled her to her feet. When he took off running for the house, she tried to keep up. Gunshots rang out, and she screamed in terror. Her nightmare had come true.

Bullets whistled by them. Through the fear holding her in its clutches, she heard Jake swear. That was enough to make her pump her legs harder. The lights on the porch grew brighter as they closed the last few yards. When they reached it, the sound of sirens made her spin around.

The police!

Before she could appreciate their arrival, Jake pushed her inside the house in front of him. He disappeared and returned with his shotgun. She gulped at the sight.

Is he going back out there?

"Stay here," he instructed.

Her throat closed up. A part of her wanted to ask him not to go, not to risk himself, but the words refused to come out.

He hesitated at the door, his gaze locking onto hers. "I'll be back as soon as I can."

She barely heard him over the hammering of her heart as he left her there alone.

* * * *

Jake

Jake had seen Dillon's vehicle arrive, and knowing his brother was here, he'd had to check on him. But when he reached the SUV, he was gone.

Maybe he pursued the shooter on foot. If so, Jake hoped Dillon found whoever was firing at him and Blair.

He was debating which way the man had likely gone so he could go after him when his brother reappeared.

"Jake," Dillon called from a small grouping of pines by the road.

"Yeah, I'm here." He started walking toward his brother. "Did you get the shooter?"

"No," Dillon spat. "He got away—silver Mercedes."

Jake closed his eyes, taking a deep breath before exhaling. "Well, at least we know this wasn't random. Where's the cruiser you sent over? How come he didn't respond to this?"

Dillon's eyes pinched with sadness as he explained, "He's dead, Jake. The shooter got him first. His body's over there." His brother pointed in the direction he'd chased the shooter.

Jake's mouth soured on a curse. This was a small town, and it was rare they'd lose an officer to a gunshot wound. "I'm sorry, Dill."

"Where's Blair?"

"The house."

"Good. Go back there. I'll come down when I've got this taken care of."

Jake hesitated. He'd been deputized by the sheriff's office and had served as an auxiliary deputy a handful of times. He wanted to help his brother but hated leaving Blair alone.

"Okay." He ran a hand through his hair and nodded, finally agreeing to let Dillon handle it. Right now, Blair needed him more.

CHAPTER 14

Jake

Jake's chest grew tight when he reentered the house. Blair was in shock. She stood rigid in the spot where he'd left her. Her eyes were unfocused, and her breaths were coming too rapidly.

He hadn't wanted to leave her, but at the chance of helping catch the bastard who'd shot at them, he'd had to. He'd wanted to ensure there was no chance the shooter would come after her again. Unfortunately, his going back out hadn't mattered.

I should have stayed with her.

Jake berated himself as he led Blair to the sofa. Needing to calm her down, he helped her recline on it, then propped a pillow under her legs.

Kneeling beside her, he softly spoke, "Blair, you're safe. It's all right. Dillon is here, and he's handling the situation. Just breathe." He rubbed her clammy hands together and tried to lower her anxiety level.

"Jake?" She looked confused, as though noticing he was there for the first time.

"I'm here. You're safe. Try and slow your breathing. Can you do that?"

"My breathing?" she asked, sounding dazed.

While she stared at him, he tried to radiate calm. "Yes, you're going to hyperventilate. Breathe with me, okay? Big, slow breaths." He placed her hand on his chest so she felt the normal rhythm of his breathing. "In. Out. Good girl. Keep doing that." Relief flooded him as she started to get it back under control.

Her eyes finally cleared and focused on him. "Jake! You're shot!"

"What?" He glanced down at his left bicep. It wasn't that bad, but it had started to really bleed. The blood had dripped all the way down his arm and covered his shirt sleeve.

"It's just a graze." He shrugged, then winced as the gesture made the pain worse.

"Let me look at it," she demanded with a stern frown.

He was impressed that all traces of the panicked woman she'd been moments earlier were gone.

She didn't wait for his permission but reached for him and explored the wound. There was a definite rip in his shirt sleeve where the bullet had torn through it. Thankfully, it hadn't penetrated, but there was a lot of blood.

"We need to get this cleaned up," she told him.

"There's a first aid kit under the sink." He led her back to the master bathroom and tried not to wince at the state of it. Two days' worth of towels littered the floor and toothpaste decorated the sink. Usually, he kept it tidier than this, but she'd interrupted the flow of his life over the last few days. Hoping she didn't notice, he rummaged through drawers in the vanity until he found the little red bag.

Blair grabbed the kit from him and made him sit on the toilet. "Take off your shirt," she instructed.

Jake obliged her. The flannel was toast anyway. The entire left sleeve was soaked with his blood. When he glanced down at the wound, he frowned. It did look kind of bad. Hopefully, it wouldn't need stitches.

"Where are the washcloths?" she asked him.

He pointed at a drawer, and she found a couple. Then, she wet one and used it to wipe the blood away. After she cleaned his arm, she gently patted the wound dry with another cloth. He was touched that she was trying not to hurt him.

Didn't stop it from stinging, though. Fighting a hiss as she dabbed on antiseptic, he ground his teeth together.

Once she had him cleaned up, she placed a dressing on the wound from the first aid kit. "I think that's all right."

Avoiding his gaze, she busied herself with tidying up. "It wasn't very deep. I don't think it'll require stitches."

Needing her on so many levels, he grabbed her hand and forced her to look at him. The way she'd pulled herself out of the panic and focused on the practical task of fixing him up was remarkable.

She had to be scared, but she didn't let it paralyze her.

There was strength beneath that polished exterior, and he admired her for it.

"Jake?" Her eyes searched for something in his. "Can I trust you?"

"You're asking me that now?" Her sudden show of vulnerability caught him off guard.

"Answer the question," she demanded.

"Yes. I'm all in, Blair." He cupped her cheek with his good arm and added, "I'm not going to let anyone hurt you."

Her eyes revealed her surprise at his response. She stared at him, and he didn't guard his feelings for once, letting her see what she'd come to mean to him. It didn't matter how much time had passed. She'd pierced his heart from the start.

Before she could speak, Dillon called for them and ruined the moment, leaving Jake wondering what her response would have been.

She broke his gaze, and he answered his brother, "We'll be right there!"

* * * *

Blair

They joined Dillon in the living room. His drawn face told Blair whatever news he had wouldn't be good. Jake seemed to agree because he grabbed her hand and squeezed it as they settled on the sofa.

"Start from the beginning and tell me what happened," Dillon requested.

They took turns relaying their view of the shooting.

"This looks like it was a targeted attack." Dillon shifted on his feet, his expression pained when he admitted, "The shooter wasn't apprehended. We know he's driving the silver Mercedes, and we've put out an APB on that. But it's likely he'll change vehicles." He hesitated before tagging on, "We lost the officer that was watching the house. We're going to have two patrols stationed outside in case the shooter comes back."

Her stomach dropped at the news, and she felt sick. Someone had died trying to protect her. And whoever was after her was still out there.

Dillon started to leave and shook his head. "I forgot. The reason I was coming over here tonight was to ask you if Trevor had any contacts in Asia. Chicago P.D. found some papers in his apartment they thought might be a lead. Do you have any idea where he might have gone over there?"

Considering it, Blair frowned. "You think he left because he stole the money?"

Dillon scratched at his neck. "It's certainly suspicious."

While Jake squeezed her hand reassuringly, Blair tried to think through five years of memories.

"Oh!" She jumped up. Perhaps she did know where Trevor went. Her hands flapped with excited waves as she explained, "Trevor always said Malaysia would be a good place to hide money. I thought he was joking, of course, but what if he was serious? We always talked of visiting Kuala Lumpur."

"It's worth looking into," Dillon suggested. "I'll contact Chicago." He clasped Jake's left shoulder, making him wince. "Sorry." Dillon looked sheepish. "Do you want a paramedic to look at that?"

Jake shook his head. "It's fine. Blair cleaned it up, and it doesn't need stitches."

"If you're sure . . ." Dillon trailed off. "Call me right away if there's more trouble or you think of anything else."

She followed as Jake led Dillon to the front door. Before his brother left, he gripped his arm. "Wait, Dill, the horses."

"I'll take care of it," Dillon assured him.

"Thanks, brother." Jake grabbed him in a bear hug, and she knew his thanks weren't only for the horses.

They released each other, and Dillon waved goodbye to her. As the door closed behind him, the weight of their situation settled on her shoulders, heavy enough to crush her.

CHAPTER 15

Jake

Blair was crying when Jake returned to the living room after hunting down some painkillers. Silent tears slid down her cheeks as she stared out the window at the police cruisers parked for their protection.

"I've trapped us here," she lamented when he got close.

The regret in her eyes unnerved him. "No. This isn't your fault, Blair." He stroked her arm in reassurance. "Besides, it's more like a staycation." He grinned, attempting to lighten the mood she was in.

Her smile didn't reach her eyes. "Right."

Seeing what she needed, he pulled her in for a hug. When she held onto him, it was clear she needed a release from the stress of the last few days. There was so much tension trapped in her rigid form.

After several minutes of rubbing her back while he held her in his arms, she loosened up as if some of the stress had melted away.

With a soft sigh, she looked up at him. "Thank you," she murmured.

Jake stared down into the liquid pools of her eyes and felt himself falling. She might've only crashed into his life a few days ago, but that didn't matter. When he splashed into the warm liquid of her gaze, he knew he'd do anything to keep her in it because he had feelings for her. It had been more than a physical connection from the start. She was his—his to protect and his to . . . *love*.

He cupped her face, and she seemed to sense the change in him because he felt her pulse quicken under his palm.

Leaning down, he placed his lips on hers. The kiss was long and sweet. When Blair opened her eyes, he saw she wanted, even needed more.

"Jake," she breathed, "take me to the bedroom."

He smiled, more than happy to oblige her. Without waiting another second, he swept her into his arms and carried her to bed.

* * * *

Blair

Blair stared up at Jake, admiring his sharp jawline and the way his hair flopped over his forehead.

He needs to cut it.

She lifted the dark strands in her hand and pushed them behind his ear. When he smiled down at her, her heart danced in her chest. She enjoyed the way he carried her in his arms as though she weighed nothing. He was so strong, this man she was falling for.

Not only physically. She'd seen so many sides to him in such a short time. It made her want to hold onto him . . . for good. To see where this relationship might lead. She'd been surprised by what he'd told her in the bathroom. Knowing he wanted to be there for her was enough to let her guard down.

Of course, she'd broken her own rule and fallen for another man. But Jake wasn't just any man. He was trusting and generous, and his love for his family and farm made him all the more appealing.

A blush stole across her cheeks as she realized she'd told him to go slow, then asked him to take her to bed all in the space of a day. But everything she felt made it seem like the timeframe didn't matter. *This* was what love was. Not whatever she'd thought she'd felt for Trevor. Her ex certainly never would've taken a bullet for her.

But Jake—brave, loyal, loving—Jake *had*. It was both thrilling and frightening that he was willing to get shot at protecting her. Seeing the wound in his arm clarified things for her. They'd been lucky because it could have been a lot worse than a mere graze.

She squeezed her arms around his neck and wondered if he cared for her the way she'd come to care for him. Her heart swelled at the idea that he might.

When they reached his bedroom, Jake dropped her on the bed. She giggled as she bounced and found him grinning down at her. His bed was a king, and the sheets covering it were soft as satin.

She ran her hands across them, loving how they felt against her bare arms. When she noticed the way Jake stared at her movements, she stopped. The primal look, as if he could devour her with just his eyes, made her pulse trip faster than a racehorse crossing the finish line.

Her core responded as she sat up and lifted his t-shirt off. He helped her then she slid her hands across his broad, hairless chest, admiring the muscles that trembled at her touch.

With him, she felt both strong and powerful. Smiling at that, she kissed her way down his stomach and thrilled at his shudder when she slid her hand down the front of his jeans.

Blair unbuttoned them, but before she freed him, Jake stopped her.

"Not yet," he told her as he lifted her shirt off.

He hummed in approval and lowered his mouth to her chest. Slipping his tongue under her bra, he teased her nipple. As a wave of heat shot straight to her middle, she couldn't help but gasp.

Jake unfastened her bra and cupped her breasts in his rough palms. The contrast drove her wild, and her skin flushed with arousal. The fire he created was alive within her, and it was burning through her defenses. She wasn't used to surrendering, but with Jake, it felt natural.

He lowered his mouth and sucked. Sensations flooded her senses, making her close her eyes on a moan. Then he was nibbling and sucking until she felt herself vibrating beneath him. She rocked against his erection and unwittingly ignited the slow burn that had been building within him.

When he disappeared, she groaned in frustration. Blair sat up and saw that he'd freed himself of his jeans. Wide-eyed, she barely had time to drink him in before he sent her soaring.

He tested her heat with his fingers, and she fell back onto the bed, closing her eyes in wonder. Then, he teased her until she was desperate to feel him inside of her, whimpering at his touch.

"Blair," Jake's voice was strained when she opened her eyes and stared up at him.

The reserved man she'd first met was gone.

Was it only days ago?

Then, she'd thought his light gray eyes cold, but now, as she gazed into their warmth, she'd do anything to protect him.

"I'm falling in love with you," Jake told her.

Her eyes widened in surprise, but before she had a chance to respond, he slid into her. She cried out as the blaze he'd built consumed her.

She wanted to lose herself in it, but his eyes held her captive. They moved together, thrust for thrust, her breathing coming in quick puffs of air. Her internal furnace was about to blow. Pleasure built inside her until she could no longer contain it. It burst out of her with a scream she barely recognized as her own.

When her body shuddered, she took Jake with her, and their combined release roared through them.

He collapsed on top of her. After her breathing finally

slowed, she savored the feel of him, wrapping her legs around his waist. He grunted, shifting up and rolling over. When he pulled her down on top of him, she rested her head against his chest and listened as his heartbeat pounded. It made her chuckle inwardly. They had certainly both gotten a workout.

And Jake said he's falling for me.

The memory of his words bloomed inside her. Even though it happened quickly, she was confident about what she felt in her heart.

"Jake"—she rose up on her elbow in order to see his expression—"I'm falling for you, too."

He kissed her. Not a kiss of passion but of love. There was no desperation in it now, only joy.

She nestled into the crook of his arm and sighed in contentment. As he held her close, she fell asleep in his arms.

* * * *

Colt

Colt cursed. Mr. Soldano wouldn't be pleased. He'd meant to kill the farmer and would have if the damn horse hadn't gotten in the way.

As for the other cop showing up, he couldn't do anything about that. That was just bad timing. But now he'd had to change cars.

Colt knew the officer had seen the Mercedes and would be looking for it. It was a good thing that jacking cars was child's play. He'd already stashed the Mercedes and procured a new vehicle.

The real problem was now they knew he was watching them.

Colt snarled. The cops would put extra patrols on the house. He needed to snatch the woman and fast if he was going to salvage this.

CHAPTER 16

Blair

Blair awoke with a start from another nightmare. In it, Jake's wound hadn't been merely a graze. She'd helplessly stared as he'd bled out in front of her.

The thought of him being seriously injured or worse—dying to protect her—scared her beyond measure. Someone had already lost their life because of her. She wouldn't let this wonderful, caring man be next. His family would be devastated if that happened.

Blair glanced at him now, resting soundly beside her. No, she couldn't be the cause of that. If she really cared about him, she'd leave. Because she wasn't just risking Jake's life anymore. It was his brother's, even his mother's. Family like Jake had—their relationship—it was too rare and too precious.

She wouldn't be the reason that got ripped away from him. A sob bubbled up in her chest, but she choked it down. She had to leave. She couldn't stomach anyone else dying because of her.

Marco's men were after *her*, not Jake. He was only in danger because he wanted to protect her. But it was her turn to protect him.

No more hiding and waiting.

What she needed to do was lead Marco's men away from Rolling Brook.

With her resolve fortifying her emotions, she kissed Jake softly on the lips, careful not to wake him. Slipping from bed, she headed for the guestroom.

After grabbing a few essentials from her luggage with hands that shook, she stuffed them in her purse. The suitcase would slow her down, so she wouldn't take it with her. The rental car was still at the bed and breakfast, and the cruisers out front would notice if she took Jake's truck. She'd have to go on foot.

Or horse.

She could walk to the stables and take the mare into town. It wasn't far, surely; she could manage that. Then she'd leave the horse at the bed and breakfast and retrieve her car.

After she had more time to think about how to word it, she'd write Jake a note. She couldn't stand the thought of him coming after her because he didn't know why she left.

I need him safe.

She crept lightly out the back door and headed for the stables. It was difficult to see the path in the little bit of moonlight the sky offered. She picked her way carefully, deciding to wait until she was far enough away from the house before she turned her phone light on because she didn't want there to be any chance the cruisers would see it and stop her.

As she walked, she felt her heart breaking.

What will Jake think when he finds me gone?

Blair hoped he wouldn't hate her for leaving. She'd done it out of love, after all. His family and the farm needed him, and she wouldn't let this nightmare deprive them of the best man she'd ever known. What remained of her heart wouldn't survive his death.

She turned her flashlight on as she neared the stables. Lost in her thoughts, she didn't hear someone come up behind her until it was too late.

There was a prick in her neck, and she spun around.

The man from the diner. Blair realized right before her lids closed, and she fell limp into his arms.

* * * *

Colt

Colt carried the woman to the black SUV he'd procured and tossed her in the back seat. She'd made his job laughably easy, sneaking out of the house like that. He didn't know what her plan had been, but it was changed now.

He chuckled and drove away from Whiteford Farm, traveling to the outskirts of Rolling Brook. The sedative he'd given her wouldn't last long, and he needed her contained before she woke up.

Good thing he had the perfect spot in mind. Mr.

Sinclair had come in handy for getting familiar with the area. He'd told Mr. Soldano about an abandoned steel mill that Colt steered toward. It would work as a place to stash the woman.

While he drove, he pondered that blackmail did have its pluses, even if he preferred a more . . . *forceful* approach.

* * * *

Jake

When Jake woke up, the bed beside him was empty. He frowned. Had Blair gone back to the guestroom? He'd hoped she'd spend the night with him.

Smiling into the darkness, he thought of his other plans for her besides sleep. Throwing on pants, he went in search of her.

She wasn't in the guestroom, but her luggage was. He scratched at his chin. Maybe she'd gone to the kitchen for a snack. They'd never had dinner, and his stomach was letting him know how empty it was.

But when he checked, she wasn't in the kitchen either, making him good and worried.

Where did she go?

She wouldn't just leave, not after what they'd shared. He dialed Dillon's number, nearing a state of panic.

"What's happened?" his brother asked immediately.

"She's not here, Dill. I woke up, and she was gone. What if they took her? We have to find her. I can't let them hurt her." He growled his thoughts with all the anguish he felt ripping at his chest.

"I'm on my way," Dillon assured him and disconnected.

Jake got fully dressed and threw cold water on his face in an effort to calm down. He had to go look for Blair.

The cruisers!

When he remembered, he ran out of the house to talk to them. One of the officers had to have seen her if she left. Outside, he noted his truck was still in the drive.

So she has to be on foot.

Jake rushed past it and knocked on the first cruiser's window. The officer inside jumped. Tonight, it seemed extra dark outside. There was very little moonlight for illumination, and the officer hadn't noticed his approach.

Recognition flared on the man's face as he stepped out of the vehicle. "Mr. Redland. What can I—"

"Where's Blair? The woman that was here. Did you see her leave?" His anxiety left no room for pleasantries.

The officer shook his head. "No one has come out that door or up this drive."

"Where's the other patrol?" His voice cracked in desperation.

The officer pointed toward the main road and Jake took off running.

The second cop saw him coming and got out of the car when he approached.

"What's going on, Jake?" It was Luther, Janet's son. He'd always liked the kid.

"Blair's gone. Did you see her leave or anyone come in this way?"

"No, neither. There's been nothing all night. If she's on foot, she can't have gotten far," Luther suggested.

"Dillon's on his way, but I'm going to start searching for her." He turned to walk away.

"Jake, wait! Does she have a phone?"

"Yes! Can you track it?" Hope flared in his chest.

"Not from here. I'll call it into the station."

He nodded and tried to focus on the fact that they would find her.

CHAPTER 17

Blair

Blair groaned. Her head was splitting. She opened her eyes, and at first, she was confused by the unfamiliar surroundings.

Where am I? How did I get here?

Looking down, she saw her hands and feet were tied to a chair. Her heart rate skyrocketed, and she struggled against the ropes.

The man!

Her head popped back up, searching for him in the darkness. Where had he taken her?

"Ah, I see you're awake." The man from the diner stepped in front of her, and moonlight glinted off the knife he held in his hand.

"Who are you?" The forcefulness in her voice belied the anxiety she was trying to distance herself from. Giving in to it would not help her get out of this situation.

"You don't need to worry about that," he told her

mockingly. "You just need to tell me where the money is."

"I didn't steal any money," she screamed at him.

"Wrong answer." He nicked her right ear with the knife.

She winced at the pain. "I'm not lying. It was Trevor. He's trying to frame me."

"Interesting," the man commented, "but you're only saying that to try and save your own skin." He nicked her other ear.

"It's true! I'd never steal from Mr. Soldano."

"Ah, so you do know the money I'm talking about." He grinned at her menacingly and made a shallow cut next to her right eye. "Why did you skip town then if you didn't steal it?"

"I didn't. Trevor and I broke up. I only left to clear my head for a few days." She was crying now but continued through the tears, "Trevor's the one that skipped town. He's gone. The police said the apartment was cleared out. He took the money, not me." Her breathing came in shallow gasps as blood dripped down her face.

The man frowned at her. "You better not be lying to me, lady, or you won't like the consequences."

"I'm not," she told him bravely, despite the fear that was trying to overtake her.

"We'll see about that," he sneered. Then he left her there, stepping outside to make a phone call, she presumed.

* * * *

Jake

Jake had nearly paced a rut in the lane in front of the patrol cruiser by the time they got a response about Blair's phone.

"They said it's here, Jake. She's on the farm," Luther told him.

He breathed a little easier for the first time since he'd found her gone. "Then I'm searching on horseback."

Luther nodded. "Dillon's bringing the dogs. We'll be right behind you."

He ran for the stables. If Blair was still on the farm, then it was possible she'd only gone out for a walk.

She would be okay. Maybe this was all an overreaction on his part.

Sliding on something, Jake lost his footing and tumbled hard to the ground.

"What the hell was that?" he growled as he jumped to his feet.

Looking down to see what had tripped him, Jake froze. It was a cell phone. He picked it up; it was Blair's. The flashlight was still on, so he shined it around to see if she was anywhere close by.

"Blair! BLAIR!" he called for her but got no answer.

The light glinted off of something else on the ground next to where the phone had been. Jake picked it up. It looked like the cap for a needle.

What the hell?

His gut turned to stone when he realized what it meant. "Dammit, dammit!"

Someone had her. Someone had taken Blair. He made

his shaking hands dial Dillon's number to relay what he'd found.

"Dill, he took her. The bastard drugged her and took her. Bring the dogs and meet me at the stables."

He hung up before Dillon had a chance to respond and got to work saddling a blue roan so he'd be ready to track down Blair as soon as his brother arrived.

CHAPTER 18

Jake

Dillon called a halt when the K-9 unit led them to the abandoned steel mill on the outskirts of town. They had nearly the entire police force of Rolling Brook at their backs and didn't want to tip off the abductor to their presence. At least not yet.

Jake dismounted and came to stand beside his brother. "She's in there?"

"It's possible," Dillon told him. "But we have to make contact with the abductor to be sure. If he's holding her hostage, we'll need to call in the county SWAT team to assist."

Jake's adrenaline pumped through his veins; he wasn't in the mood for more waiting. "The woman I love is in there, Dill. I can't sit here and do nothing."

His brother grasped his arm. "I know. But if you charge in there, you put her more at risk. There's a protocol for these situations, Jake. Let me use it."

He stared Dillon down. Logically, he knew his brother was right. Still, emotionally, he was in agony at the thought of Blair spending even a minute more as that bastard's hostage.

"What do we do?" Jake conceded.

"Make contact." Dillon gestured the other officers over. "Okay, form a perimeter around the building. I want eyes on all possible exits. I'm going to make contact with the abductor, verify our hostage is in there."

They scattered to take up their posts.

"Luther, call for SWAT. I want them ready if we need them." Dillon turned to Jake. "You stay with me."

Jake nodded, biding his time for now. He'd try Dillon's way, but nothing would stop him from going in after Blair if it didn't work.

* * * *

Blair

"Well, it seems you weren't lying about Trevor. He did skip town," the man informed Blair, running the knife lightly across her left cheek. She held her breath, waiting for the pain when it bit in.

"That means your part in this is done," he told her as he placed the knife against her throat instead. "Unless you want to tell me where Trevor went?"

His face was mere inches from hers, and the look in his eyes told her he meant to kill her. They gleamed with pleasure at the thought of slitting her throat.

Whether she gave him Trevor's whereabouts or not, he

wouldn't let her live. She opened her mouth to tell him to go to hell when the sound of Dillon's voice echoing through the mill interrupted her.

"This is the police. We have the mill surrounded. Come out with your hands up."

"Well, that changes things," her captor mumbled with a curse. He pulled a gun from the back of his pants and flashed it in her face. "Try to run, and you're dead," he threatened as he began to cut her restraints loose from the chair.

Hope that she might yet survive made her legs twitchy, but once he freed her, the man held the gun to her temple. With the cold steel pressed to her skin, Blair bided her time, letting him march her to the mill entrance.

* * * *

Jake

Jake's stomach dropped at the sight of Blair's bloody face, and the gun pressed against her head.

He started to race forward, but Dillon stopped him. "This is what we wanted, Jake. We know she's alive."

He gasped for air, "For how long?" His heart was in his throat, and he had to choke past it to get the words out.

Instead of responding, Dillon addressed the man holding Blair hostage. "Let Miss O'Rourke go and—"

"What?" The man interrupted. "You'll let me go? I don't think so, officer. Here's what you're going to do if you want to keep her alive."

Jake growled.

"Ah yes, farmboy," the bastard addressed him, "if you don't want any more of her pretty face carved up, you better tell the cops to cooperate."

"What do you want?" Dillon asked before Jake could respond.

"I want to walk to my car without you putting any bullet holes in me, and I want to leave without being followed."

"You know I can't let you do that," Dillon told him.

"Then it seems the pretty little lawyer is staying with me for a while," the man jerked Blair's head back by her hair, and she yelped.

"You better not touch her, you bastard," Jake yelled with all the rage burning through his gut.

The asshole laughed while he retreated with her inside the mill.

"God, Dill, did you see her face?" Jake choked out. "I told her I wouldn't let anyone hurt her." His eyes were tortured as they pleaded for a way to fix this.

Dillon tried to reassure him. "She's going to make it, Jake. We've got SWAT coming in. Look, it's the same bastard I chased off the farm last night. He knows he can't go anywhere right now, and he won't kill her. She's his insurance policy."

"How long?" Jake asked.

"30 minutes, an hour tops."

He nodded, but he couldn't wait that long. "I'm going to check on the horse."

Jake felt Dillon's eyes on him as he walked away. His

brother was worried, and he had a right to be. There was no way he'd wait around for SWAT. If there was a chance he could get Blair out of there now, he had to take it.

CHAPTER 19

Jake

The crumbling building that used to be the old mill was built in the early 1900s. It had underground tunnels that once diverted water to run the mill's equipment. Jake doubted Blair's captor knew about them.

He swiped a rifle from a patrol car, cursing himself for not bringing his own weapon. He'd been so focused on finding Blair that little else had penetrated.

The tunnels were about ten feet across and half that in height. He hunched over and tried not to knock his head on the ceiling. At least the rifle had a scope with a light on it. Turning it on, he used it to illuminate a couple of feet in front of him. It was eerily quiet, apart from the constant sound of water trickling down the stones.

Jake worried that any misstep would echo in the rooms above and give his position away. He trod as softly as possible until he neared the end of the tunnel and found it opened into a machine room. Creeping to the entryway, he checked around the side of the door to see what lay beyond.

She's alive.

His breath caught with relief. He'd found Blair.

She was tied to a chair, and the man who'd taken her sat next to her, playing with a switchblade knife. The man's back was to Jake, but he wouldn't risk shooting from this angle on the possibility the bullet would go through him and into Blair, or worse—he'd miss the man and hit her.

Her eyes went wide when she noticed him. Jake shook his head at her, hoping she understood not to give him away.

I need the bastard to move away from her.

He attempted signaling Blair with his hands, asking her to make the man move, but they didn't get a chance to try.

The asshole must have noticed her staring at something because he spun around and stood up. "Well, well, farmboy." He pointed his gun in Jake's direction. "Better come out from behind the door for the lady's sake."

Jake cursed and stepped out into the line of fire. "Look, the cops don't know I'm in here. Let me have Blair, and I'll tell you how to get out of here unnoticed."

"Ah, ah, ah," the man chided. "I'll make the demands. For starters, put down that rifle."

Jake hesitated, knowing that once he did, the man would shoot him. He'd be no help to Blair that way.

"Jake, don't!" she pleaded.

The man moved behind her, placing his knife against her throat. The other hand still held the gun on Jake. "Now!" He sneered with the order.

"Wait!" Jake put the rifle on the floor. "I know a way out for you."

"Tell me."

"Let her go first." He inched his way toward them.

"Stop! Come any closer, and I slit her throat."

Jake froze. Tears ran down Blair's face, making tracks in the blood dried there. He understood she thought this was hopeless and that one or both of them were going to die.

Not if I can help it.

He held both hands up, imploring the bastard, "Look, let her go. You can have me as a hostage. The cop you were talking to out there? He's my brother. I'm a bigger bargaining chip. Let her go."

"Noooo!" Blair wailed. "Don't do this. I was trying to keep you safe." She sobbed harder. "And you walked right into danger. Your family and the farm need you. You can't do this."

Shock rippled over Jake at her words. *Did she mean . . . she left to protect me?*

The man chuckled. "Yep, that's right. She made snatching her very easy leaving the house like that. Stupid woman"—he shrugged—"but I don't need both of you." The man raised the gun higher and pointed it at Jake's head. "Tell me how you got in here."

He looked at Blair. She was staring at him with fear in her eyes. "I love you." He hoped like hell that wasn't the only time he'd get to tell her that.

"That's touching, really. Tell me, farmboy, NOW! Where's the way out?"

Jake's stomach clenched as the man pressed the flat of the knife further into Blair's throat. He wouldn't tell the bastard anything until he let her go.

Facing down the gun, Jake racked his brain to come up with a scenario that worked in their favor. If only he were closer, he could overpower the man. For that, though, he needed a distraction.

Before he even finished the thought, they got lucky. Dillon came sneaking in behind the shooter.

Jake needed to keep the man's attention on him so Dillon would be able to get close enough to take the man down.

"Okay, I'll tell you," he started. "Look, this is an old mill, right? They used to run things on hydroelectric power. Obviously, you need water for that. Where do you think they got it from? Had to pipe it into the building somehow. There's a tun—"

He didn't need to finish as Dillon grabbed the man from behind. His brother knocked the gun out of the bastard's hand and threw him to the ground face-first.

Jake watched as Dillon twisted the arm with the knife, and it fell to the ground. The move was one all police recruits learned during their first week of training because it worked without fail.

Knowing they were saved, he raced to Blair and started untying her bonds as his brother cuffed the shooter.

Dillon pulled the man up and pushed him toward the entry. "I'll deal with you next," he barked at Jake as he passed.

He knew he'd screwed up, but he didn't care about that right now. All he cared about was the fact that Blair was safe.

Kneeling in front of her, he cupped her face in his hands. Her eyes were clear, and he was once again impressed by her ability to quiet her fear.

"Blair, I'm so sorry he hurt you." He clenched his jaw so tight it ached as he stroked her cut cheek.

"He didn't, not really," she assured him. "You stopped him before he had the chance." She moved her arm up to grip Jake's hand and winced. The ropes had cut into her wrists, leaving the skin raw where it had burned through.

He glanced down, and his eyes froze over. He wanted to kill the bastard for doing this to her. Clamping down on his rage, Jake lifted Blair carefully into his arms and carried her outside. The sun had risen while they were inside the mill.

Dillon approached. "Dammit, Jake! What were you thinking?" he yelled. "You almost got yourself killed. You're lucky I remembered those tunnels when I noticed you were gone."

It took a lot to get his brother riled, and he had a right to be, but they had bigger things to take care of right now. "Dillon, Blair needs help." Jake's eyes pleaded with his brother to see past the anger.

"Right, take her to the paramedics." Dillon waved in the direction of the ambulance.

Jake nodded a thank you and carried her away.

136 Blye Donovan

CHAPTER 20

Blair

Blair felt relieved the cuts she'd received weren't deep enough to scar. The rope burns were painful but superficial as far as wounds went, the paramedics had assured her. They would heal in six to ten days and leave no traces.

Jake called his brother over as they finished patching her up. "So, who is he?"

"Jeremy Morelli—nicknamed Colt. He works for Soldano."

Blair was glad Dillon's anger had cooled while he'd focused on his duties as the on-scene commander. She didn't like being the cause of strife between him and Jake.

"He's talking then?" Jake asked, sounding surprised.

"Not a lot, but he gave us Sinclair. We'll get *him* on conspiracy charges for providing information on the farm."

"The bastard," Jake snarled. "I knew he was dirty."

Dillon nodded. "We'll go after him. He won't be bothering you about developing Whiteford anymore."

"And Soldano?" she asked softly. Her throat was sore from crying, but she needed to know Marco wouldn't be sending more men after her. Jake must've sensed her unease because he squeezed her hand.

"We've got Morelli on grand theft auto, kidnapping, and murder. He'll talk and give us Soldano or he's not getting off any time soon." Dillon clasped her other hand. "I'm sorry this happened to you."

She forced a smile. "Thank you for saving us."

Dillon hugged her. "I had to. You're family now." He smiled as he released her.

She glanced at Jake and noticed the smirk on his lips at Dillon's statement. He put his arms around both of them in a bear hug, and she squeezed them back.

Relief that Jake had survived lifted the weight from her heart, though the air was still thick with tension over the night's events.

"Dill, if we're done here, I'm going to take Blair home," Jake said as he released them.

His brother raked a hand through his short hair, nodding. "I've got phone calls to make."

"JAKE! DILLON! Oh my God, are you all right? I just heard what happened! This is crazy! It's straight out of *Chicago P.D.*!" Daisy came running toward the group while gasping her questions. She didn't slow down when she reached them. "I can't believe it was the guy from the diner!" She noticed Blair and paused. "Oh, Blair." She gently rubbed her hands. "I'm so sorry. Are you okay?"

"Daisy, we're all going to be fine," Dillon assured his sister. She glanced at him and burst into tears. Daisy dropped Blair's hands and hugged Dillon fiercely. As he rubbed his sister's back, Blair had to smile. Daisy seemed capable of being as much of a whirlwind as her mother.

After several long seconds, she gave Dillon one last squeeze and turned to Jake to do the same.

"Don't you two ever do that to me again," she demanded, but her eyes belied the anger in her voice.

It was easy to see how scared she'd been for her brothers. Family was as important to Daisy as it was to both of them. They all depended on each other, and the thought of one of them not being around for that any more was a sobering one. It was why Blair tried to walk away in the first place. To keep them whole.

Dillon's voice broke into her thoughts. "Daisy, Blair's been through a lot. Why don't we let Jake take her home? I've got to finish up here, then I'll head to the diner. Don't let rumors spread. I'll fill you in on everything later. But the bad guy is in custody, and no one else was hurt, all right?"

She nodded with a smile full of relief. "All right, brother, but you better tell Mom and Dad. You don't want them hearing about it from someone else first." She gave Blair a hug and Jake a kiss on the cheek. "Stay out of trouble, you two. Wouldn't want anything else to ruin the possibility of a summer wedding." She winked at them and left for the diner.

Blair stared after the bubbly raven-haired woman—too astonished to comment. It was a good thing Daisy hadn't waited for a response.

Really, a summer wedding?

She glanced sideways at Jake. He was grinning after his sister.

Dillon cleared his throat, breaking the silence. "Rock, paper, scissors?" he asked Jake.

"Not a chance, Dill. You're the cop. It should come from you." He grinned at his brother. "Besides, I've got to take Blair home. You can tell me how that call went later."

He reached for her hand, and Dillon scowled. "Fine," he called after them, "but you owe me."

Jake turned and waved his acknowledgment.

Dillon was right. They *did* owe him. She was happy the news he had to report to Jake's parents was better than it could have been. She didn't want to think about how Dillon would have handled it if he hadn't gotten to them in time.

She shivered against a ripple of fear.

Thank God his parents would hear they were all alive and well.

Thinking of Jake's parents, she realized they'd have to explain everything to his mother now that the threat was gone. She hoped Sandy would forgive her for lying.

Blair tugged Jake to a stop. "We have to tell your parents everything at dinner on Sunday."

He looked at her as if unsure why she was telling him this now. "Uh-huh. We will. Sunday. No big deal."

"No big deal! What if your mom hates me? Won't she be mad that we lied?"

"Blair"—Jake cupped her face in his hands, rubbing

his thumb gently across the bandages—"you only lied to protect her. She'll understand that." He kissed her softly on the lips. "I love you. They will, too."

Her chest filled with warmth, burning away the worry and making her smile. "I hope so."

Jake grinned. "They will."

He tugged her forward, and her steps felt lighter as she followed.

When they reached the spot where he'd tied his horse, Jake asked, "How 'bout some breakfast? I'm starved."

Instead of answering, she stared at the roan. "Is this how we're getting home?

When he nodded, she had to chuckle. "My knight in shining armor."

His answering smile said he was happy she felt up to teasing him. "Something like that."

"Are we going to ride off into the sunset?"

"Hell no. I need food, a hot shower, and you, not necessarily in that order." He winked at her, making her laugh.

He hadn't lost his sense of humor even after what they'd been through. He was still her Jake, and she was determined not to let the events of last night make her a victim.

I'm stronger than that.

"Well, I'm glad you haven't lost sight of what's truly important," she goaded.

Grinning, Jake bent down and kissed her forehead, nose, bandaged cheek, and lips. The fire was there, but it smoldered without burning her now.

Blair savored the way his touch built the flames within her and kissed him back with all the love she felt. He was hers, and she was his. Nothing else mattered now.

Except maybe breakfast. When her stomach growled loud enough to startle the birds in the trees, they broke apart laughing.

Jake mounted the horse and reached down for her hand. She climbed up behind him and wrapped her arms around his waist. He threaded his left hand through hers and hugged her closer to his back, careful of her bandaged wrists. The way he always took care of her made her sigh with contentment.

"Ready?"

She nodded, then realized he couldn't see her. "Yes!"

He urged the horse forward with his legs. "Take us home, Blue."

Blair smiled at his words. She had a home here now *and* a family with Jake. And Dillon and Daisy. Perhaps she'd open a law practice in Rolling Brook.

Because despite everything that had happened, she'd gained those things, home and family. She wasn't a victim but a victor. The thought bolstered her enough to face the days ahead.

She closed her eyes and rested her cheek on Jake's back. "I love you," she whispered.

Of course, he heard her. "I love you, too, Blair. Forever and always."

EPILOGUE

Two Months Later

Trevor

Trevor sensed that someone was following him. He glanced over his shoulder repeatedly as he ducked and dodged vendors on the crowded street. His business in Kuala Lumpur was complete, and he was looking forward to retiring to Tahiti.

Glancing behind him again, he stumbled, and strong arms jerked him upright. Before he knew what was happening, he'd been spun around and handcuffed by a man in a dark suit.

"What! What is this? What are you doing? I'm an American citizen," he shrieked.

More men in suits surrounded him. They were Asian, but Trevor didn't think they were from the Royal Malaysian Police.

"We're very aware of who you are, Mr. Preston." The man who'd handcuffed him spoke with a hint of a British accent. "You're under arrest for money laundering, embezzlement, and tax evasion. Shall I go on?"

"I want a lawyer!"

"You'll get one, I'm sure," the man told him. "Once we extradite you. Of course, these things take time. You'll be confined until then."

Trevor gulped. Confinement was not part of his plan. "I have money! I can pay you. You don't need to take me in. We can work something out, please!"

"We'll have to add bribery to the list of charges." The man smiled. "Please go on, Mr. Preston. You're incriminating yourself quite well."

Trevor collapsed to his knees as his world tilted on its axis. "No, please, I can give you names. Crime bosses in Chicago, shady businessmen, dirty politicians. Please! Just let me go!"

"I've heard enough." The man with the faint British accent cuffed him on the head. "You can save that for the Americans."

Trevor sniveled as the men from Interpol led him away, explaining to him that he'd be extradited to Chicago and held accountable for his crimes.

* * * *

Blair

"They got him," Dillon announced. He'd come out to the farm to tell them the good news in person. "Trevor was in

Malaysia like you thought." He smiled at Blair.

She breathed a sigh of relief; the last scene of the nightmare she'd lived through was coming to a close. The man who'd abducted her was in prison. He'd given Dillon what they needed to go after Marco Soldano, who now awaited sentencing. After everything the police had been able to pin on him, Blair knew it would be a heavy one. They'd even pushed for Chase Sinclair's arrest on conspiracy charges. The developer had been willing to do anything to get Jake off his land, and now he'd pay the price.

"That's great, Dill!" Jake exclaimed, pulling her back to the moment. "Thanks for letting us know." He gave his brother a quick hug.

"I'll have to go to Chicago to testify." Unconsciously, she swiped at the spot, high on her cheek where Colt had cut her. That battle was still ahead of them.

Jake grabbed her hand and squeezed. "We'll go together."

She smiled at him. They would. There'd be no more of one of them trying to protect the other. They'd finish this together.

Glancing down at the ring on her left hand, she told him, "Together."

And once it was done, they'd celebrate their new beginning together. She had to chuckle to herself.

Daisy was right about that summer wedding, after all.

BOOKS BY BLYE DONOVAN

Rolling Brook Protectors
Hunted at Whiteford Farm
Gifts from a Stalker
Small Town Frame-up
Condemned by Secrets
Marked as Queen of Hearts

Stand-alone Novels
Undercover Santa
Blaze of Glory

Texas Heat Shared Series
Wait for You

TOP Security Series
Going Rogue
Being Bold

A NOTE TO READERS

If you enjoyed this book, please consider leaving a review. They help spread the word about my books through the recommendation process and help new readers decide if my books will be a good fit for them. Reviews also contribute to my rankings on sites like Amazon, making my stories more visible to new readers. Even a one-line review makes a difference!

If you can't get enough of Rolling Brook or the Redlands, pick up *Gifts from a Stalker* to read Dillon's story! He's got some demons to face, and Lydia is the right woman to help him do it. But she has her own past to contend with, not to mention fending off Dillon's advances. Because falling for a client is forbidden . . . isn't it?

If you'd like a free novella set in the Rolling Brook world, subscribe to my newsletter. By signing up, you receive an EXCLUSIVE book featuring a woman on the run and forced proximity with a troubled military hero.

Want more updates, teasers, and giveaways? Follow me on social media.

All my links can be found here: https://linktr.ee/blyedonovan.

Thank you for reading!

xoxo,

Blye Donovan

ACKNOWLEDGMENTS

I wouldn't be a writer if I hadn't first been a reader, so I'd like to thank all the wonderful romance authors who have come before me and whose books introduced me to the genre, sparking a love interest that continues to this day.

My husband, whose support means more than I can say. Thank you for that and for being a sounding board and brainstorm partner for new ideas.

My family and friends—Heather, Cheryl, Angie, and Kate—thank you for reading through the rough drafts of my first-ever novel and providing feedback. I am very grateful for the time you gave me. Your input helps me be better at my craft.

Lastly, thank you to everyone who read *Hunted at Whiteford Farm* and loved it. I hope this updated version does that original manuscript justice and that you enjoyed Jake and Blair's expanded love story!

ABOUT THE AUTHOR

Blye Donovan is a military brat and a veteran who resides in the Lowcountry of South Carolina with her husband and fur-child, Maximus. Besides books, she's addicted to coffee, peanut butter, and shoes. When she's not feeding these addictions, she writes books that are romantic suspense stories featuring strong heroines and alpha protector heroes overcoming dangerous villains. Her books are often set in small towns because she loves the atmosphere associated with them, especially  when they have historic architecture. She was supposed to become a historic preservationist, but . . . writing has always been her passion. You can check out her current series, follow her on social media, and more all at this link: https://linktr.ee/blyedonovan.

9 798986 768304